A Foundation of Fear

Kim McMahill

This is a work of fiction. Names, characters, places, and incidents either are the product of the author's imagination or are used fictitiously, and any resemblance to actual persons living or dead, business establishments, events, or locales, is entirely coincidental.

A Foundation of Fear
COPYRIGHT 2019 by Kim McMahill

Contact Information: titleadmin@pelicanbookgroup.com

Cover Art by *Nicola Martinez*

Prism is a division of Pelican Ventures, LLC
www.pelicanbookgroup.com PO Box 1738 *Aztec, NM * 87410

The Triangle Prism logo is a trademark of Pelican Ventures, LLC

Publishing History
Prism Edition, 2019
Paperback Edition ISBN 978-1-5223-9855-4
Electronic Edition ISBN 978-1-5223-9854-7
Published in the United States of America

Dedication

To my wonderful and supportive husband, Jim. He shares my passion for adventure and exploring the world, which is where I get ideas and inspiration for my novels. Thanks to my mom for being my number one fan and the most persistent marketing advocate I could hope for.

BOOKS BY KIM MCMAHILL

Risky Research Series

A Dose of Danger (Book 1)
A Taste of Tragedy (Book 2)
A Foundation of Fear (Book 3)
A Formidable Foe (Prequel — free micro-read)

Other Novels
The Lodge
Marked in Mexico
Shrouded in Secrets
Big Horn Storm
Deadly Exodus

ONE

Sweat soaked her light pink, *I Love DC* t-shirt. Hip hop music blasted through her earbuds, helping to keep up her energy level as she pounded down the trail in Rock Creek Park. She ran nearly every night year-round, hot or cold, rain or shine, but with her boss on the road, the past couple weeks at work had been busier than usual. Now she was paying the price.

With only a mile and a half between her and her car, tension already gripped her lazy legs. No one ever said running was easy, otherwise everyone would be doing it, and the trails would be packed with people. As it was, she hadn't come across another jogger for over fifteen minutes, and the knowledge made her uncomfortable. The park was generally well-used, especially this time of year when the temperatures were pleasant. The hive of activity always gave her a sense of security, but tonight the lack of people encouraged her to run a little faster.

The thick foliage on the deciduous trees crowding the trail made the early evening seem darker than it actually was. As she rounded a bend, she spied a jogger ahead and exhaled a sigh of relief. The tall muscular man's pace was slow, so she shortened her stride to avoid catching him.

Comforted at no longer being alone in the vast park, she settled into a modest pace and let her thoughts drift back over her work day. She had started to worry that her boss, and the owner of the company, wasn't happy with her performance, despite her hard work and long hours. Then out of the blue, her boss called with an apology and an invitation to lunch.

She loved her job with the prestigious lobbying firm and after investing several years, she possessed no desire to look for another. She had found her passion in life. Thankfully, the communication from the owner earlier in the day removed a huge burden from her mind.

The trail curved, and the jogger in front of her disappeared. When the trail straightened again, he was no longer in view. The straightaway was long enough that she doubted he could have gotten far enough ahead for her to lose sight of him, especially at the speed he was jogging. No benches lined the path, nor could she spy any side trails. He had vanished.

The vegetation was dense and a haven for biting bugs, so she couldn't imagine anyone venturing off the maintained trail, especially as the light waned. Stopping her music and pulling the bud out of her ear, she listened. Silence, except for the chirping of hidden insects, ruled the early evening.

She looked around and located nothing unusual. An uncomfortable sensation of being watched made her shoulders shudder. Picking up her pace, she struggled to visualize where she was on the path, trying to determine if it would be a shorter distance to her car if she turned around or kept going on the loop trail. Deciding she was somewhere near the halfway point, she forged on.

Just as she decided her paranoia had gotten the best of her, the sound of running shoes hitting the hard-paved surface caught her ear. She glanced over her shoulder but saw no one. She tried not to let her imagination run wild, but the man couldn't disappear. If he wasn't ahead of her, he had to be behind her. Close enough for her to hear him. This time the thought of company on the trail didn't bring any comfort.

Fishing her cell phone out of the small pocket in her running shorts, she clenched the device in her fist, making her feel less vulnerable. *Should I call someone and let them know where I am?*

She dismissed the thought and kept running. Another half mile passed with no incident. She began to relax, chastising herself for her moment of weakness. She had lived in large cities her entire life and knew dangers existed, but seldom let those possibilities influence her activities.

Focused on her fumbling attempt to reinsert the earbud to get the music flowing, she almost collided with the person who stepped out of the brush hugging the trail. She tried to dodge the man, whom she was certain by his attire was the same one she had been following earlier, but he grabbed her upper arm and yanked her toward him. She dropped her earbud and cell phone as pain shot toward her wrist. She struggled to think clearly, knowing she needed a plan, but the fear of dying pushed all ideas from her mind.

He spun her around so her back was pressed tight against his hard chest. With one of his arms firmly across her neck, she couldn't see his face. The increasing pressure on her windpipe made it difficult to breathe or to scream out for help.

She tried to kick backward at his shin, but he was too close for her to inflict much damage, and the futile attempts only made her lose her balance. Squirming and struggling, she tried to pry his arm away from her throat with her free hand, but his grip was like a vise.

His stranglehold tightened. Desperation and lack of oxygen clouded her thoughts. A vision flashed through her mind of all the things she had yet to do and all the people who would miss her, encouraging her to keep fighting to free herself from the man. She didn't want to die. Not this way. Not in the prime of her life.

She scratched frantically at his bare skin, but doubted her stubby fingernails were doing any damage to his thick-muscled bicep. The attack didn't seem like an opportunistic random act of violence. Her assailant clearly knew what he was doing. He held her in a position that limited her options at self-defense, and his arm across her throat made it impossible to scream for help or plead for her life. If she did manage to get away, she had yet to see his face, so would be unable to identify him.

The more she fought, the more her strength waned. As darkness threatened to overtake her, the sensation of being dragged off of the paved pathway pushed its way into her barely conscious mind. She vaguely registered the need for a weapon. Her vision blurred. She reached for a low hanging tree branch. Her hand missed its target, and all went black.

TWO

One week later

Margaret Blair was exhausted. In an attempt to save the weight loss company she had built from nothing, she'd existed on only a few hours of sleep a night for the past week. The manufacturer for the prepackaged, nutritionally-balanced meals to support the Maggie Blair Diet Program had shut down without notice, leaving her scrambling to come up with a new supplier, and her legal team working overtime on damage control.

She could think of a million other ways she'd rather be spending her Friday night than reading the latest status report. The news was grim. The company's survival was precarious at best.

The in-house medical advisory board and registered dieticians, along with outside independent consultants and scientists had spent the past week poring over the data on the sweetener in order to advise her on how bad the situation could become. The company's legal team focused on assessing the potential lawsuits likely to arise from current clients who consumed products which might contain a dangerous sweetener.

Margaret and the rest of upper management had been searching for a manufacturer that possessed the ability and capacity to step in and get the flow of meals back on track as quickly as possible. Her public relations team was working on damage control. She'd have to give them all a healthy bonus if the company survived.

She removed her reading glasses, clicked the mouse to close the report which had been e-mailed to her, and rubbed the bridge of her nose. It seemed they were making progress on mitigating damages, but whether or not they could recover was yet to be seen.

"You look like you could use a break."

The sound of her husband's voice split through the churning of ideas surging through her mind. She looked up and smiled. Urban was not only her husband of twenty years and business partner of nearly as many, but he had been her rock during the past week's turmoil. He had put in nearly as many hours, yet he looked as handsome, confident, and as in control as ever.

"Yes. I probably should eat something, and a glass of wine would definitely help ease the tension."

Margaret stood and moved from behind her massive mahogany desk, rotating her neck in an attempt to work out the kinks.

"We'll get through this. We've lost nearly thirty-five percent of our clients with the Giant Cactus Foods recall, but we'll get them back. I have faith the products A & C Foods will be producing for us by next week will be comparable in taste and effectiveness

"Oh, Urban, I hope you're right. You know how much this company means to me. When I opened my first gym nearly two decades ago I dreamed about expanding to provide complete health and nutritional services for women and men. I never imagined we'd create an empire. The thought of losing it is almost too much to bear."

Urban reached for his wife and pulled her into his arms.

"I know, and I hope you realize I would do anything to save this company. I've always done whatever it takes to make it successful. My priority hasn't changed since the day we met. All I want to do is make you happy. If that greedy fool who cut corners to pad his pockets wasn't already dead, I'd kill him myself." His grip tightened until Margaret squirmed.

"I'm sorry. I hope I didn't hurt you. It just makes me so angry that we could lose so much because of someone else's actions."

Margaret stepped out of his embrace and retrieved her purse and coat. She paused while he helped her into her jacket. She turned and smiled. Wrapping her arms around his neck, she placed a warm kiss on her husband's lips.

"I feel betrayed. We put a lot of faith and money into that company and look where it got us. We must put the anger aside for now and deal with the consequences, though I would love to make someone pay for this disaster. If I ever find out that anyone else has contributed in any way to this debacle, he or she will regret crossing my path."

"I have no doubt, darling. Let's go enjoy a nice relaxing dinner and try to put this all behind us for a few hours." Urban flipped out the lights and escorted his wife to the elevator.

THREE

Devyn Nash's ribs still ached and pain shot up from the soles of her feet with every step she took. Only a little over a week had passed since she had chased a killer through cactus-covered desert at night in her bare feet. If that wasn't enough, she had leapt off a rock ledge and tackled the fugitive, which in hindsight probably wasn't a smart move. She had desperately wanted answers, not another corpse. Unfortunately, things seldom turned out as planned.

She struggled to mask the pain as she made her way across the bustling room crowded with the desks of her fellow FBI agents in the Salt Lake Field Office. Halfway across the room she spied her partner, Nick Melonis, concentrating on his computer screen.

Stylishly dressed as usual, and not a wisp of his dark slicked-backed hair out of place, Nick was her complete opposite. Devyn ran her fingers through her long blonde strands, still damp from her morning shower, and tried to coax some order to the tangled tresses.

They had been partners for a little over two years, longer than she had been able to keep any other partner—which surprised everyone in the bureau, including herself. Nick wasn't only her partner, but he had become a good friend.

Contrary to many of their fellow agents' beliefs there was nothing romantic between them. In fact,

Nick was about to remarry his ex-wife, which couldn't make Devyn happier. She absolutely adored Morgan Hunter, and they had become quick friends, much to Nick's displeasure, which only added to Devyn's happiness.

Spotting Agent Joe Gardner approaching, she wished she was closer to Nick and the support he often provided. Nick had taken on the role of big brother, and she appreciated that he always had her back at work, and more recently, in her personal life. Agent Gardner, on the other hand, went out of his way to push her buttons. She feared one day she would snap and take a swing at him which would likely get her suspended. Slugging a fellow agent was seriously frowned upon by her boss and the bureau.

"Hey, Nash, heard you crashed Nick's party in Arizona."

She looked toward her partner, shooting daggers with her eyes at the back of his head.

"Whoa, not from Nick. I had an interesting talk with your buddy in Phoenix, Agent Bob Tanner, on Friday. I couldn't wait until you got into the office this morning."

Devyn groaned. In a weak, overly-medicated moment she had let a tidbit about her personal life escape to Agent Tanner of the Phoenix FBI Field Office while they were wrapping up a case together.

"He seems to think you have a man in your life."

Devyn ignored Gardner and kept walking. She doubted he'd take the hint and get lost, but Nick had been encouraging her to walk away and count to ten before responding to any comment she deemed to be stupid.

"Come on. You can tell us. I mean it's almost too

farfetched to believe since you hate men."

She was only on eight but couldn't resist the bait. She stopped and slowly turned. "I like Nick, Fitz, Gordo, my dad, our boss, and until he gossiped like a thirteen-year-old girl, I had even considered forgiving Tanner for ditching me on a remote country road during the Cocaine Canyon Operation. It's just you I don't like."

"Ouch, but that doesn't answer my question. Who's the lucky guy? Anyone here? Anyone we know?"

"Save it, Gardner. We've got work to do."

Nick's calm, yet stern statement sent Gardner back to his desk. Nick's good timing was one more asset she appreciated about her partner.

"I hope you uncovered something new on the Risky Research case or have identified any of Coterie's members and didn't just say that to get rid of Gardner," Devyn replied. "I won't get a decent night's sleep until we catch those creeps and put them behind bars where they belong."

"I agree, and actually I do have some information. Tanner got the autopsies and toxicology reports on both victims in Arizona. No surprises. He confirmed one froze to death and the other was poisoned. And after talking to Stan Jacobson's neighbors again and going through more camera footage and the original investigation reports, Tanner's pretty convinced Stan was murdered. The case has been reopened with the Phoenix FBI in the lead. Unfortunately, the prime suspect is dead."

"Aren't you full of cheery news this lovely Monday morning? None of that gets us anywhere. It only confirms what we already suspected. I'm getting tired of reacting and cleaning up bodies. We hit brick walls everywhere we turn, and it seems like we're just waiting for the next victim to show up. We've got to figure out who's behind Coterie and stop them."

Devyn winced as she lowered herself into her chair. She wasn't a morning person and not overly fond of Mondays. She hated being less than one-hundred percent physically and wasn't a patient person.

The doctor confirmed her ribs were cracked and the only cure was time. Her feet weren't in much better shape. The medics in Arizona had pulled out as many of the cactus spines and slivers as they could, but the rest would have to work their way out over time. To top it off, her second weekend back home in Salt Lake had not turned out at all like she had hoped.

"I figured you'd be in a little better mood this morning since Sheriff Gage Harris dropped in from Wyoming to pay you a visit," Nick whispered.

"I tried to convince him to postpone, but he showed up anyway. He made me soup, took me for a drive up into the mountains, refilled my prescriptions, pulled newly exposed slivers out of my feet and rubbed numbing antibiotic ointment on my soles, tucked me in at night, and made himself comfortable on the couch. It definitely wasn't how I pictured our first weekend together, and I wouldn't be surprised if it was our last."

"You two just can't catch a break."

Devyn had first met Gage Harris when they worked together on a counterfeiting case half a decade ago. The attraction was immediate, but they'd never gotten together. Then, a few months back, the spark got rekindled when they were reunited during the

Uinta Vitamin case in Wyoming. But again, they hadn't had the chance to move forward. She'd thought this weekend would be the opportunity they needed.

"Now you're so banged up you can't enjoy the romance. Hopefully, you weren't as bad of a patient as I would expect."

"Tell me about it." A man moved toward them, and Devyn signed. "Oh, not now. I'm not in the mood to be nice."

Nick looked over his shoulder. "Be gentle," he urged. "For reasons unknown to any of us, he continues to be your biggest admirer."

Devyn tried to smile as she watched Gordo, the FBI's young technology guru make his way toward their adjacent desks with a plate in hand.

"Hi, Devyn, I heard about what happened in Arizona, so I asked mom to bake a batch of your favorite brownies," Gordo said as he set the plate on her desk.

Devyn peeled back the plastic wrap and grabbed a square slathered with peanut butter frosting and sunk her teeth into the decadent treat. As she savored the flavors and registered the compassionate look in Gordo's puppy-dog eyes, her earlier anger faded.

"Delicious. Thanks, and tell your mom thanks. These are so good it almost makes me forget about all my aches and pains."

"Glad you like them. If you need anything else, let me know. I can drive you places, help you with groceries, you just name it."

"Appreciate the offer, but I'm good. I'm moving around a lot easier every day."

"You know where to find me, in the lab, which is where I need to be heading or Fitz will be mad." Gordo hustled off.

Devyn looked over at Nick. "I know. I've got a problem, but I don't want to crush the kid."

"Don't tell me Gordo's your man," Gardener stated as he walked up and grabbed a brownie off the plate. "Poor kid has no idea what he's wishing for. You've brought stronger men than him to tears."

"You flatter me. Now get out of here. If you touch these again, you'll lose a finger." Devyn snatched the plate out of his reach.

"That's the charm all the men love," Gardner mumbled as he walked away licking the frosting off his fingers.

Devyn poked another brownie in her mouth, leaned back, and closed her eyes. When she opened them, she realized Nick was watching her. She pushed the plate toward him. "You can help yourself."

"Don't let Gardner get under your skin."

"I can't help it. When a woman reaches my age and has never been in a serious relationship, she can't help but question herself. It can't be the entire male population, so it must be me, right? To have Gardner reminding me nearly every day that I'm the agency pariah and a man repellent doesn't do a lot for my self-esteem. I can hold my own in the field against any guy, and I've effectively put in his place every lecherous pig who thought I should just jump into bed with him. Apparently, that makes me an evil shrew."

"No, that makes you good at your job and an even better judge of character. There's nothing wrong with having morals. Gardner's a jerk."

Devyn's phone rang. She took the short call and returned the receiver. "Our boss summoned us to his office. I guess that means I have to stand up now."

She grimaced as she hoisted herself out of her chair.

"I'm not as fond as you might think of watching you suffer, so I'll share something with you that will make you smile. You gotta keep it between the two of us, though," Nick said.

"You've got my word," Devyn replied, excited by the thought of Nick finally sharing something with her that she didn't have to pry out of him.

"I did give Gardner a black eye for stealing my gnome."

Devyn laughed, even though it hurt her ribs. "Thanks. That makes my day. Hope you're still feeling sorry for me when we get to Conroy's office."

"What did you do, Devyn?"

"I pulled Senator Carson Grant's voting record for the past five years, shortly before the Gen Tech Medical and Pharmaceutical Research Lab explosion since that's the first incident we believe may be linked to Coterie."

Nick shook his head and smiled, which surprised Devyn. The last time she questioned the senator, she and Nick nearly got suspended. But, after almost losing the love of his life to Coterie, Devyn suspected Nick was as determined as her to track down and bring the deadly group to justice, no matter whose cage they had to rattle.

FOUR

Sofia Wilks couldn't remember ever experiencing a worse week, and the unpleasant activities continued. She had returned from a very disappointing and traumatic job to learn that her assistant, Justine, had been killed while out jogging. She had talked to her earlier the same day and was thankful the exchange had been a friendly one.

Justine's murder hit her hard. Maybe she was going soft or maybe the tragedies were starting to get personal. First her mentee, and now the best assistant she ever had had been taken from her in the prime of their lives, leaving her feeling alone.

Since Justine's family lived on the west coast, Sofia had been called in by the authorities to identify the body, putting her closer to law enforcement than she cared to be. Luckily, no one made the connection to any of her aliases from previous assignments.

She had worked in many capacities under many different names, including most recently, Janice Green and Candace Rogers. Now, she needed to find a way to be herself, at least for a while, before she forgot who she wanted to be altogether. She wasn't all too sure who that might be anymore. She had lost her direction in more ways than one.

The identification of Justine's body haunted her. She had looked peaceful despite the bruises around her neck and the bloody stubs on her hands. The medical examiner divulged that there had clearly been a struggle, and that although the killer had likely cut off her fingertips to remove any DNA evidence from under her fingernails he was still able to retrieve some from the bottoms of her shoes and tissue on her neck.

Sofia couldn't erase the images of the brutality or the medical examiner's words from her mind. There were much less ruthless ways to kill someone, like poisoning or freezing a victim to death.

After the autopsy was finished and the body was released, Sofia made arrangements to send Justine's body to her family in Los Angeles. Later in the week she would fly out to attend the funeral. She hated to fly. Not only did she risk being tied to one of her aliases, but enclosed spaces made her claustrophobic and often allowed painful childhood memories to invade her thoughts.

Her phone buzzed, and she picked it up.

"Yes, Trevor," she hissed through clenched teeth.

"Your 2:00 PM appointment is here. Should I send him in?"

"Give me five minutes."

Hearing Trevor's voice only sharpened her sorrow and anger at losing Justine. He claimed he had nothing to do with her death, but the timing of his arrival indicated otherwise. He had been sent by J.R., the head of Coterie, to replace her assistant before she was even aware Justine was gone.

Why would J.R. be so intent on having his man inside my operation that he would go to such lengths to remove Justine?

She possessed no proof J.R. had ordered the hit or that Trevor was the hitman. When she confronted J.R., he stated the tragedy was likely a random crime in a big city. She wasn't buying it.

J.R. claimed Trevor had been sent to protect her and the timing was an unfortunate coincidence. She had never needed anyone's protection, and she didn't believe in coincidences. She didn't trust Trevor, whether or not he had anything to do with Justine's death. If he truly didn't kill Justine, she suspected that he knew who did, and that person was still out there. There was nothing more dangerous than not knowing your enemies.

Forcing the thoughts from her mind, Sofia went to her private bathroom and checked her hair and makeup. A few quick touchups and she was ready to face her next client who wanted her company, Buyers Choice Foundation, to lobby to do away with the "do not call" list, like it was much of a deterrent anyway with all of its loopholes.

Returning to her desk, she opened the file she had prepared on Mr. Tucker. A quick perusal and she felt adequately prepared to schmooze. She pushed the button on her phone.

"Send Mr. Tucker in."

The door opened. She stood and smiled at the middle-aged, balding business man in an expensive blue suit approaching her desk. She extended her hand in greeting while flashing a warm smile. Taking her hand, he gave it a limp shake, making Sofia cringe.

"Have a seat, Mr. Tucker, and tell me what Buyers Choice Foundation can do for you to help keep capitalism strong and thriving in this great country of ours."

The line worked every time. The man beamed at the opportunity to legitimize his desire to harass people in their homes in the name of freedom to conduct business and provide consumers with endless ways to spend their money. He wouldn't be concerned about those citizens' freedom to enjoy an uninterrupted dinner with their families.

People like him sickened her, but she could name her price, and he would happily pony up. He was a parasite like so many she came into contact with in her line of work, sucking the life out of hard-working Americans, harassing them until they often gave in and quit fighting the bombardment of high pressure sales tactics.

Even though she didn't like him or his kind, she could relate on some level. She took great satisfaction in manipulating the political and free-market systems in her favor and playing the game better than everyone else. The thrill of winning often trumped the gratification achieved from the resulting profit.

FIVE

Margaret perused their client list data. Another two percent had cancelled their membership over the weekend, but at least the mass exodus had slowed. When the news first broke about the potentially dangerous sweetener used to manufacture their food products, they had lost five percent of their members each day the first week.

Now it was time to rebuild client confidence in their program, which was much more than just food. The complete plan included a personalized diet, health and fitness counselors, mobile apps to track food intake and exercise, and of course, pre-packaged nutritionally balanced meals and desserts shipped to clients' homes. The food portion of the plan was by far the biggest profit center and the one currently in jeopardy.

Maggie Blair had switched to Giant Cactus Foods, or GCF, as it was commonly called, nearly two years ago. She should have known it was too good to be true. The cost was low, the health claims were remarkable, and the products were delicious. Luckily, she had a naturally thin frame, so after testing a number of the products she continued with her regular, mostly all-natural diet. Give her a salad and a small piece of grilled fish or chicken and she was content.

Her mind wandered back, struggling to remember the details of the transition to GCF from her previous supplier. She recalled being thrilled with the substantial increase in the profit margin, but her husband had handled all the negotiations. At the time, she thought he was a business genius, but now she wondered how thoroughly he had vetted the company.

"What has you so deep in thought, darling?" Urban asked as he entered Margaret's office.

"Just thinking back to those days two years ago that are ultimately responsible for this mess we're in right now."

"There's no point trying to second guess anything, dredging up the past, or attempting to place blame. What's done is done, now we must focus our energies on moving forward," Urban replied.

"I can't help but feel responsible. I'm usually involved in every decision, but I was so caught up in the price and potential, I didn't do my own research."

Urban swallowed hard and took her hand. "If anyone is to blame, it's me. I thought I'd done ample checking into their performance record and had received several positive recommendations, but I too was blinded by all the benefits."

"Who recommended them?"

"Does it really matter at this point?"

"Yes, I most certainly will never take advice from that person or persons again, and if there is any way I can return the favor at some point, I will," Margaret stated as she held her husband's gaze, waiting for an answer.

~*~

Urban was pinned into a corner, and he wasn't

sure how to extricate himself. How could he confess to his wife that he and the deceased President of Giant Cactus Foods, Preston Hoyle, were both members of an organization few were aware even existed?

He hadn't known that the sweetener was dangerous but assumed the company had no issues with cutting corners, falsifying records, or doing whatever it took to make a huge profit. They all did; it was just business. After learning about the sweeteners amazing attributes and low cost, Urban had wanted in. The early success made his wife happy and his marriage strong.

His mind reeled, trying to think of a reply. The look on his wife's face made it clear that she wanted an answer, and she wanted it now. She wasn't a patient woman and could be vindictive, so he had no doubt she wanted to punish someone for her losses.

"With everything on my mind right now with trying to save the company, I'm drawing a blank on the names. I remember discussing Giant Cactus Foods with a couple of guys at the club. One has since died, and the other is out of the country, I believe."

"I want the names. Try to dig them up."

"I likely lost the contact info when Jean converted my old rolodex to an electronic contact list. I asked her to clean it up."

"Well, try to remember. I'm sure the names will come to you if you focus."

"Anything for you, my love, but I've got to go. I'm late for a meeting with the lawyers to discuss their review of the new A and C Foods Company contract," Urban replied as he prepared for a hasty retreat.

"Wait, I'll go with you. The last time I disengaged with supplier negotiations look what happened. It came back to haunt us."

Urban nodded and waited while Margaret called her executive assistant to rearrange her schedule. The more progress he made on rectifying this situation, partially of his making, the closer he came to losing what really mattered—his wife.

SIX

Devyn tapped timidly on Special Agent in Charge, Gerald Conroy's, door.

"Come in."

Devyn looked apprehensively at Nick before twisting the knob. "After you," she stated as she stepped back and motioned for Nick to enter.

Nick strode confidently into their boss's office with Devyn at his heals.

"Sit," Conroy stated.

Devyn and Nick obediently took seats across the desk from their boss.

"Nick didn't know I pulled Senator Grant's voting records," Devyn blurted out in an attempt to spare him any disciplinary action she might receive for digging into a topic she had been told to avoid in the past.

Conroy held up his hand to silence her.

"Things have changed since I ordered you to stay away from Senator Grant. We now have an open investigation into a number of pharmaceutical, research, and nutritional incidents that were previously classified as accidents until the tragedy in Wyoming shed light on Coterie."

Devyn let out the breath she had been holding and relaxed her shoulders. By the tone of Conroy's voice, she doubted suspending her was on the morning's agenda.

"When I learned you were looking into Grant's

voting record, I decided to do a little digging on my own."

"Did you uncover anything?" Devyn asked, scooting to the edge of her chair.

She had come into her boss's office expecting to be reprimanded. To learn that wasn't going to happen and he was actually looking into the senator himself sent a surge of adrenaline through her veins, making it difficult to sit still.

"I didn't discover any solid evidence that Senator Carson Grant is in anyway involved with Coterie, but I think he merits a closer look. As you are aware from your investigation, he has used his position as the Chair of the Senate Committee on Health, Education, Labor, and Pensions in some interesting ways. He's pushed for questionable approvals, lobbied his fellow senators to relax drug regulations, and he's blocked every attempt to cap drug prices. Most recently, it seems he's trying to prevent the merger of two small weight loss chains. What's interesting about this piece of information is that these two small companies are trying to merge in order to compete with the larger companies. One of the largest is Maggie Blair, Inc."

"No," Devyn exclaimed. "Maggie Blair is one of three companies who used Giant Cactus Foods to produce their pre-packaged foods for their diet plans. Needless to say, all of these companies are struggling to survive the fallout from Giant Cactus Foods' use of a deadly sweetener. Their clients are cancelling in droves, and there will no doubt be hundreds if not thousands of lawsuits."

"The senator blocking a merger of small businesses hoping to compete with a large corporation that had been using Giant Cactus to manufacture its products could be a coincidence, but I thought it was worth checking out."

"So, are you saying the ban on investigating Senator Grant has been lifted?"

"Unofficially, yes, but Nash, be discrete."

Nick coughed, disguising a laugh. He flinched as Devyn kicked his shin.

"Discretion, it is. First, we'll dig further into the business relationships between Giant Cactus and the companies they manufactured frozen foods for, especially those that may not survive the crisis. According to the news, one of those companies is independently owned and the other two have publicly traded stock, which has plummeted. If any of these companies know anything maybe they're mad enough to talk unless they're in bed with Coterie too."

"We're also following up on a few loose ends from Arizona tied to the Risky Research case," Nick added.

"And?" Conroy asked, rolling his hand in a motion to hurry things along.

"We're trying to figure out what the connection is between Aaron Truscott, the guy Devyn chased through the desert in bare feet and jumped off a cliff to tackle in Arizona, Coterie, and Candace or Janice or whoever she is. We think Aaron could be a key. He was working for Giant Cactus Foods and apparently knew Candace, so we have to assume that the deceased president of the company, Preston Hoyle, Candace, and Aaron all have ties to Coterie or at least to each other."

"If they are all tied to Coterie they clearly aren't very loyal to each other," Conroy stated.

"I've been trying to wrap my mind around why one member would murder her colleagues. I imagine that once Aaron was captured, he became too big of a liability. He could have exposed them all, which was why I went to such great lengths to try to keep him alive. Morgan didn't think very highly of Preston Hoyle or trust him at all during her short tenure in his employ, so maybe Coterie didn't trust him with their secrets either," Devyn replied.

"Well, whatever the connection, I hope we can turn up something solid before anyone else dies," Conroy muttered. "Get after it and keep me posted."

Devyn and Nick nodded, quickly stood, and left their boss's office.

"That went better than I expected," Devyn said once they were out in the hallway.

"Yes, but you don't need to try to protect me, Devyn. I'm with you all the way on this one even if it costs my career. These greedy thugs almost stole everything from me, and I won't rest until they're all behind bars or dead."

SEVEN

Sofia sorted through the mail in her in-box on her desk. Justine used to open, sort the incoming mail, and deal with anything that didn't need Sofia's personal attention. Handling this task herself was time consuming, but Sofia wanted to limit Trevor's access to as much of her company's information as possible until she could figure out a way to get rid of him, short of killing him.

She had pleaded with J.R. to remove his goon, but he sounded offended that she would reject his attempt to protect her. He asked her to give Trevor a chance in a way that sounded more like an order than a request. She didn't want to give Trevor a chance. His timing and personality were equally unsettling, and if J.R. cared enough about her to provide protection, how come she hadn't seen him since Phoenix?

The door opened, and Trevor strode into her office. He looked more like a secret service agent or an assassin than an executive assistant with his slicked-back dark hair, arrogant posture, intimidating expression, and his muscles straining the sleeves of his dark blue suit. She had witnessed the wary looks from her staff and clients as they approached his desk. She understood their apprehension.

Whenever Trevor was around, her senses went on high alert. She trusted her instincts implicitly since those gut feelings had often been the only thing between life and death. At the moment, they were screaming out warnings to watch her back.

"Assistants generally knock. Since I'm sure we can agree that title is a farce, I won't bother demanding it. What do you want?"

"A truce. J.R. wants you to accept me and get more comfortable around me. I'll knock from now on."

"It's a start, but I'm afraid I'll never accept anyone who's been forced on me and who's given me no reason to trust him."

"J.R.'s concerned for your safety, don't ask me why."

"That's bull, and we both know it. Who's he been sending to clean up Coterie's messes created by incompetent men? When I found you in my office after Justine's death I thought you were an intruder. If you recall, I took you down with little difficulty before realizing you had been sent by J.R. I most certainly didn't feel protected when you were lying on the carpet with my heel in your side."

Sofia almost flinched as his expression changed instantly from passive to murderous.

His eyes bore into her with pure hatred. Red crept up his thick neck, his nostrils flared, and his fists clenched at his sides.

She refused to look away as they stared each other down.

"I told J.R. I'd try, but I have limits. My threat the day we met still stands. We can work together and hope J.R. regains his trust in you so we can part ways, or one of us could end up dead."

Sofia suspected J.R. had sent Trevor to keep tabs on her but hearing Trevor state that J.R. had lost his trust in her was a punch to the gut. She hadn't signed on with Coterie to be their muscle, and she readily admitted she was losing her stomach for all the violence and killing. She tried to hide her emotions from J.R., but clearly, he had noticed her weakness and had sent Trevor.

"Did you barge in here for a specific reason or just to annoy me?" Sofia asked, fighting to keep the tremor out of her voice.

"This came for you by courier." Trevor tossed the elegantly embossed envelope on her desk and marched out of her office.

She watched his retreating form until his broad shoulders exited, and he shut her door. Glancing down, the return address sent a sense of dread through her mind. Pulling out the antique brass letter opener with its six-inch razor-sharp blade, she sliced open the thick lined envelope.

"An invitation to his upcoming fundraiser? What's he thinking? Why would he want someone who's harboring damaging family secrets mingling with friends, family, and donors?" she mumbled as she stared at the handwritten note.

Sofia, I sincerely hope you'll join us for an evening of fine food and entertainment. Yours Truly, Senator Carson Grant.

The last time they talked she detected his confidence growing as though he believed the balance of power was shifting. It was a false sense of security he was developing since the secrets went far deeper than he could imagine. She hoped to never relive the ugliness from her childhood, but she feared he was about to force her hand.

EIGHT

After several hours of searching, Devyn came to the conclusion that there was nothing unusual about the business relationships between GCF and the two smaller companies for which it manufactured frozen entrees and desserts. She wasn't able to uncover any troubling links between Maggie Blair and GCF either, but she did learn that Margaret Blair contributed heavily to Senator Grant's reelection campaign the previous go around.

"Interesting," she mumbled.

Nick looked up from the document he was reading. "Yes?"

"Apparently, Margaret Blair of Maggie Blair, Inc., has been a big contributor to Senator Grant. Many large corporations and big businesses support the senator, so that alone isn't odd, it's the fact that so many trails continue to lead back to him. It's possible all the connections could be coincidences, and they likely are. I just can't picture the spineless womanizing politician heading up such a ruthless and well-organized crime ring as Coterie."

"I can't either, but that doesn't mean he isn't involved in some way. Maybe he's being manipulated and doesn't even realize he's connected."

"That would make more sense. Nearly every politician hides a skeleton or two in the closet. Maybe Coterie blackmails him for favors."

"I'll dig into his family history and see if I can turn up anything worthy of blackmail," Nick offered. "I was also wondering if we should make a quick trip to Denver this week and talk to Margaret Blair."

"Excellent idea if you can sell it to Conroy. My schedule is fairly open all week since the Risky Research cases are my priority, so any time she can meet with us and you can get us flights, I'll make it work."

"Agent Tanner just sent us an update on the Phoenix investigation. You can check it out while I go get approval from Conroy for a quick trip to Denver."

Devyn nodded and opened the e-mail from Agent Bob Tanner that Nick had referenced. Bob noted that when the Phoenix FBI ran Aaron Truscott's prints they got a hit on an Aaron Holmes, which she had already known since shortly after his arrest. Tanner had also uncovered that the kid was in and out of foster homes until he was fifteen. He had acquired quite a police record by then, mostly for petty theft and vandalism, and then disappeared. Aaron Holmes' juvenile records showed he dropped out of school about the time he disappeared.

"No wonder I couldn't find anything on Aaron Truscott going back very far," Devyn mumbled. Her research into Aaron Truscott revealed that seven years ago at age nineteen, he had enrolled in an Ivy League School. There was no record of him prior to that.

How would he have the grades required for admission if he didn't even graduate from high school? Where would he get the money, and who would recommend him?

Devyn jotted down a note to request his school records when she had a few minutes. *Where was he for four years between dropping out of school and enrolling in college?* Her phone rang, interrupting her train of thought.

"Nash."

"Hi, are you helping Nick teach that self-defense class tonight?" Morgan asked.

"No, what do you have in mind?"

"I thought we could organize a girl's night. You can grab a pizza or we can order out, and I'll supply the adult beverages."

"Sounds like a plan. I'll be there around six thirty," Devyn replied, thrilled to finally have a close girlfriend. The fact that Morgan was Nick's ex-wife was a bonus since she knew their friendship made him nervous.

"What's the plan?" Nick asked as he walked up to their desks and sat down.

"Morgan and I are doing a girl's night since you're tied up with that self-defense class tonight."

"I'm really regretting volunteering to teach these once a month for the next three months, but when I said I'd do it, I had no idea Morgan would be back in my life."

"And you thought it might be a good place to meet women, I'm sure."

Nick rolled his eyes. "No, I volunteered because I think it's important for people to know how to protect themselves, and unless you've forgotten, Conroy strongly encourages us to do at least forty hours of community outreach a year."

"Yep. I better figure something out soon so I don't get dinged on my performance evaluation this year."

Despite her outward grousing about the mandatory volunteerism, she had participated the past winter in teaching kids with various disabilities how to ski and had thoroughly enjoyed it. The kids were so happy to be out on the slopes, and they seemed to appreciate the experience so much that it had made her feel really good. When the program was over for the winter she had missed the kids but wouldn't admit that to anyone.

"Please behave," Nick stated, interrupting her thoughts. "What happens at works stays at work."

"I have no idea what you're talking about," Devyn replied, feigning as much innocence as she could muster.

Nick nodded his head toward the gnome couple sitting on his desk.

Devyn laughed. "Your creepy little mariachi gnome isn't nearly as pathetic now that I procured its better half from your better half."

"I'm sure I have no say in tonight's little event, so let's get back to work. I got us an early morning flight on Thursday. Margaret Blair put us on her schedule, and she seemed more than eager to talk. Did Bob forward us anything interesting?"

"As we already knew, the prints from the man working for GCF under the name of Aaron Truscott came back to an Aaron Holmes, but what's new is that Bob found a little history on Holmes."

Devyn quickly filled Nick in on what she had learned so far about Aaron's past, which wasn't much, except that the kid dropped out of school and ran away about four years before he showed back up with a new name and enrolled in college. Her curiosity about the four-year void between dropping out of high school and the foster care program and resurfacing as Aaron Truscott and attending a prestigious university was growing with every detail she uncovered.

"I'll request Truscott's university records. Hopefully, those will come back quickly and shed a little light on how a high school dropout foster kid gets into a big-time university," Devyn stated.

"Keep me posted. I need to go make sure the room is set up for tonight's class. Then I'm heading home for a bit to see Morgan and grab a bite to eat since I'll be working late."

"Hey, before you leave. I keep forgetting to ask you something. The last time I saw our buddy Agent Bob Tanner in Phoenix, he mentioned he owed you. I was just wondering what he thinks he owes you for."

"Took a bullet for him."

"You mean that tiny little scar on your shoulder?"

"I didn't say it was a big bullet, but he still appreciated the sentiment."

Devyn laughed as Nick walked away. She still had a couple hours left to work before she needed to leave in order to pick up a pizza and be at Morgan's place on time. Devyn wasn't sure why she felt nervous about the evening. Morgan was easier to be around and talk to than any other woman she had ever met, but she had never been part of a "girl's night" before and wasn't sure what was expected.

The phone rang. Looking down at the caller ID, she couldn't help but smile.

"Hello, Gordo. Yes, I'm feeling better today. No, I can't think of anything I need, but thanks for asking."

She replaced the receiver and looked up. "I'm really not in the mood," she grumbled as she watched Agents Gardner, Jones, and Thompson saunter toward her desk.

"Was that your mystery man?" Gardner asked putting "mystery man" in annoying air quotes.

"Not that it's any of your business, but no, it was the tech lab." She purposely avoided telling them it was Gordo since that was another source of their entertainment.

"We're all friends here, Devyn. You can tell us. There is no man, is there? You just told Tanner that to yank his chain and make you not look like such a hopeless spinster."

Devyn rolled her eyes. Gardner was so juvenile at times that she was surprised he was such a competent agent. She wasn't comfortable trying to convince Gardner she had a man in her life, when after last weekend, she wasn't sure she still did. Gage still called nearly every night since returning home to Wyoming to check on her, but his concern sounded more like a brother than a boyfriend.

"Since when are we friends?" Devyn asked. "I'd say co-workers, peers, colleagues, often adversaries, but friends may be stretching it a bit, don't you think?"

Jones and Thompson chuckled and Gardner turned red.

"Yep, she made him up, and told Tanner, hoping it would get back to us so we'd quit thinking she's a pathetic loser and a major man repellent." He turned and stormed away.

Jones and Thompson quit laughing.

Jones gave her a look she thought might indicate he wasn't proud of what had just happened and Thompson mouthed a "sorry."

Devyn smiled at the two agents and shrugged her shoulders. Maybe they weren't as bad as Gardener, but she still held no respect for anyone who wouldn't disagree with a bully to his face. That was the difference between men like Gardner and his cronies and men like Gage and Nick. Gage and Nick would never treat anyone, especially a woman, with such a lack of respect. Nick did all he could to diffuse the situation without forcing the whole floor to take sides, but she could only image Gage's response.

The thought of Gage made her anger over Gardner fade. She looked forward to the sound of his deep masculine voice nearly every night and hoped there was some way they could make a long-distance relationship work.

NINE

Urban hoped Margaret was satisfied with their lawyer's advice on the new contract with A & C Foods to provide frozen entrees to their clients. The sooner they could get the meals rolling again, the sooner they could put this whole mess behind them. She was a tough customer, but their options were a little limited, and time was of the essence.

"It looks like A & C Foods can do the job, and they aren't jabbing us as hard as they could under the circumstance," Margaret said to her husband as they left their legal advisor's office after signing the contract with their new supplier.

"Yes, anyone who watches the news or follows the stock market would realize they have us over a barrel. People on a diet can't just quit for weeks or months. They need to get back on track as soon as possible or we'll lose them all," Urban replied, relieved that Margaret was on board.

"Well, if their product is as close to as good as what GCF provided and they can get the meals flowing as soon as they claim, that's all we can hope for at the moment. And if they help us out of this crisis, I'll remember it."

"I'm sure you will, darling," Urban mumbled.

His wife stopped abruptly in the hallway, her arms folded across her chest. By the expression on her face, he feared she didn't like his comment, and he instantly regretted letting it slip out.

"What do you mean by that?"

"Just that you don't forget nor do you ever forgive. I'm aware of how passionate you are about this company, but there are more important things in life than money and success."

"Name one?"

All of his old insecurities from his youth came flooding back to him. How could she say something so hurtful? She was the most important thing in his life, but clearly, he rated somewhere below wealth, achievement, and the company. He wondered how far down the list he actually fell.

Both he and Margaret hailed from modest upbringings, though she aspired to a higher social status in life. She possessed the looks to achieve such success by means other than hard work if she had chosen to go that route, but she was driven and had toiled tirelessly to build an empire. He would have been content remaining a middle-class couple, but Margaret was never satisfied, she always wanted more.

They married young and were madly in love, but the more success they achieved together the more he could sense them drifting apart. He had resorted to drastic measures over the years to ensure that the financial stability she valued so highly was maintained, including allying with dangerous people. Now, some of those decisions were coming back to haunt him.

"Never mind," he said as he turned to walk away.

"Don't be childish," she called after him. "Of course, you're important to me, but we can't pay the mortgage on our ten-thousand square foot home, own a vacation condo in the Bahamas, have a personal chauffeur, a company plane, or belong to that exclusive country club you enjoy so much without money."

"Those things are only meaningful because I can share them with you. I would give it all up for your happiness."

He watched his wife struggle for a retort. She had aged well. Her skin was smooth and youthful. Her body still turned heads. Her golden hair shined like a jewel. Her pert nose was perfect for the elegant shape of her face, but her angry expression dampened her classic beauty.

Urban suspected her love for him had cooled over the years, but his had remained the same. Her family always thought she could do better, so he had dedicated himself to showing them that he was good enough for her. He still loved her more than life itself. In fact, he reluctantly acknowledged that he would not hesitate to kill for her. The realization made him shudder.

TEN

Sofia hated feeling like she needed to sneak out of her own office, but it was none of Trevor's business where she was going. She listened to his muted voice as he talked on the phone, the rustling of papers, and the annoying squeak of his desk chair.

The chair never made noise before, but then again, Trevor probably outweighed Justine by sixty pounds. Memories of Justine's cheery disposition made her sad and angry. She missed Justine and the stability the young woman had brought to Buyers Choice Foundation. The clients loved her perky and efficient assistant, and she made Sofia's time in the office seem normal, unlike the rest of her life. The foundation used to be Sofia's sanctuary. Now her business felt like a prison. Something needed to change soon.

When the noise stopped, Sofia paused for a few minutes and heard nothing, so assumed Trevor had gone to the break room for his afternoon jolt of caffeine. He clearly thought highly of himself and his abilities, but she had gotten the jump on him during their first encounter. She also already ascertained he was a creature of habit, so he had vulnerabilities. He was strong and fit, and she had probably lost any future element of surprise, so she hoped to avoid another physical confrontation with the big muscular man. From here on out, she would need to outwit him.

Sofia grabbed her purse and slipped out of the

office and headed for the park. Once she was sure she hadn't been followed, she found a bench far enough away from the nearest person to avoid being overheard. Pulling out her burner phone, she punched one of only two numbers stored in its memory.

"Why would you send me an invitation to your fundraiser?"

"Hello, to you, too. So, should I assume you're calling to RSVP that you won't be attending?"

Sofia didn't like the cocky tone of Senator Grant's voice.

"You idiot," she hissed. "It wouldn't take a genius to connect the dots if they saw us together. Some of my biggest lobbying successes can be directly tied to issues you've exerted influence over."

"There will be many lobbyists in attendance, including those who've achieved great success due to my position and assistance. Many lobbyists meet with me regularly, not just you. It's what you people do. You come to my office and try to convince me to support your causes. So what's really bothering you, Sofia?"

"That you're not worried about putting me in the same room as your mother, whom I assume will be attending."

The chuckle resonating through the line unnerved her even more. She never thought he was very smart, but he was clearly as unethical as his old man. She had no doubt he was up to something.

"Why are you laughing?"

"You're done blackmailing me. My mother knows all about my father's affairs, and she made peace with it years ago. According to her, there are more ex-mistresses out there than she can shake a stick at. If she let every one of them or their family members blackmail her, she'd never get anything done. So, tell whoever you want that your young mother, who we'll assume was a cheap gold-digging tramp, had an affair with my father over thirty years ago. Not even the tabloids are going to go after an eighty-year-old ex-politician for an extra-marital affair from decades ago."

Sofia was stunned. The senator had been such easy prey, until now. How much more would it take to keep in line? She feared there was only one way to find out.

"If only your father's transgressions ended there."

"I suppose you're going to tell me you're my half-sister? Mother said there's at least one illegitimate kid out there, so I suppose it isn't out of the realm of possibilities. Even if you can prove it, don't think you'll be welcomed into the family with open arms or that you're entitled to one cent of the family money. You don't want to tangle with our attorneys."

He answered her question in no uncertain terms. She'd have to expose so much more of her past to ensure he'd keep doing their bidding, but she wasn't sure if she was willing to share the one secret she had been carrying around for so long. The memories were too painful to toss around like a bargaining chip.

She had given so much to Coterie and what had she gotten in return? They didn't make her rich, only richer. At first, she thrived on the thrill of out maneuvering and posturing, but she was quickly tiring of the game, and she had never fathomed it would go so far. She had no problem ruining lives, but she never signed on to take them.

Sofia wasn't sure what else to say to the senator so she pressed the end key on her phone, stowed it in her purse, and slowly made her way back to the office. She needed to plan her next move carefully. Most of all, she had to decide how far she was willing to go to keep the senator on a leash. Once she played her last card, there would be no turning back.

ELEVEN

Devyn swung by the take-and-bake pizza shop and picked up her favorite thin crust pepperoni and green chili pizza and a tub of raw cookie dough that she had no intention of cooking despite the warnings on the label.

She pulled into the driveway at Morgan's place and parked her car. Nick used to live here but had moved into a small apartment when Morgan had come to town. Nick intended to stay in his apartment until their marriage. With her hands full, Devyn made her way to the door. She was thankful that Morgan had apparently heard her pull up and let her in before she had to figure out how to ring the bell while juggling a pizza in one hand and a tub of cookie dough in the other.

Morgan relieved her of the pie, and she followed her hostess into the house. She found Morgan so easy to get along with that she couldn't imagine why Nick had let her get away. In the short time she had known Morgan, Devyn's world had definitely expanded. She had never really had a girlfriend in her adult life, so she wasn't sure what a "girl's night" entailed, but what woman didn't like cookie dough?

"Great timing, the oven just reached temperature and I'm starving," Morgan said, ripping the plastic wrap off of the pizza.

"Hope you like green chilies."

"Arizona's been my second home since childhood, so yes, they're right in my wheelhouse. And I hope you aren't planning on cooking that cookie dough," Morgan said as she placed the small plastic tub in the refrigerator.

"Are you kidding? Of course not."

Devyn smiled and looked around. She had been to Nick's place many times before, but everything had changed since Morgan had come back into his life. The place was no longer as organized or as sterile. It was still uncluttered, but it now sported signs of a woman's touch. There were flowers on the table, decorative throw pillows on the couch, family photos on the mantel, and a more fragrant smell greeted her at the door.

"Red or white?" Morgan called out from the open-concept kitchen adjacent the living room.

"What goes best with pizza?"

"Beer."

"If you've got one, I'll go with a beer then."

Morgan laughed and Devyn could hear her popping the tops on two bottles. Morgan brought the bottles out, looking as elegant as ever, even in shorts and a tank top. Devyn took the bottle from Morgan and sat with her legs folded under her at one the sofa.

"How do you do it?" Devyn asked.

"Do what?"

"Look glamourous even when you're chilling out. I look like I've just finished running five miles, and you look like a million bucks, and we're both wearing blue shorts."

"Your shorts are made for jogging; mine are made for leisure. It's a totally different cut designed for specific purposes. Wearing your hair down would glam you up a bit more, though I suppose you probably wear your hair in a ponytail in case you need to take off running after a bad guy. We can go shopping sometime if you want, and I'll help you pick out some more flattering, less athletic-looking options."

"I'll probably take you up on that offer. I'm not as concerned with flattering as I am with finding a few items that'll render Gage unable to keep his hands off me. I'm getting a little tired of his old-fashioned manners."

"Be careful what you wish for. I've spent an entire business career fending off unwanted advances, so a respectful man is something to cherish."

"I know. It's just this long-distance thing is harder than I thought it would be."

"I can't wait to meet your sheriff. He must be something special."

"He is," Devyn replied. "He's tall, broad-shouldered, has this wild sandy-colored hair that I want to run my fingers through, a deep voice that sounds like a country song, great manners, and he's tough and smart."

"He sounds wonderful, though I'm pretty partial to the dark-haired, glasses-wearing, borderline metro-sexual, Type-A man."

"Nick is equally as handsome, but in a different way. He's tough and smart, too, and I've really appreciated the brotherly intervention with Agent Gardner. If it wasn't for Nick running interference, I probably would've been put on administrative leave by now for decking a fellow agent. Add the fact that he treats you like a princess, and I can definitely understand the attraction there."

Morgan sat down at the opposite end of the sofa. "Nick has mentioned the Agent Gardner situation. It makes him furious, and he wishes he could do more."

"I appreciate the sentiment, but ultimately, it's my problem," Devyn replied.

Devyn leaned toward Morgan with her bottled extended.

"Cheers! Here's to hot, respectful men, good food, and knowing Nick is grinding his teeth, worrying over what we're talking about."

Morgan laughed and clinked Devyn's beer bottle with hers.

When the timer chimed on the oven, Devyn followed Morgan into the kitchen. She discarded her empty bottle and pulled two more out of the fridge while Morgan removed the pizza from the oven, placed it on the counter, and cut it into slices.

Devyn and Morgan sat on high stools around the kitchen island and enjoyed the first slice in silence.

"I realize you can't really talk about work, and Nick doesn't say much either, but he did mention that Conroy granted you some leeway in your investigation, which you were very excited about and you both hoped this would give you the tools you needed to track down Coterie."

"Yes. Senator Carson Grant used to be off-limits. I almost got us suspended once when I approached him and started asking questions about his influence as Chair of the Senate Committee on Health, Education, Labor, and Pensions, and a connection I saw between several issues on their agenda and an incident at a medical research company. That incident was determined at the time to be a tragic accident, but I didn't buy it then and I've since been proven right.

Conroy ordered me to stand down, but now he said I could look into the Senator, 'discretely.'"

Morgan chuckled. "I haven't known you long, and no offense, but I'm not sure discretion is your style."

"None taken because you're correct in that assessment, but I'll give it a shot if it means I can dig a little deeper into the senator's past. I'm primarily interested in the issues he's backed and his contributors."

Devyn studied Morgan for a moment. She wondered if what had happened in Arizona was still bothering her, but with Nick always close at hand, she hadn't thought to ask. She was terrible at this girlfriend thing.

"I probably should have asked sooner, but with Nick around all the time I figured you two had it all handled. Are you doing OK with everything that happened in Arizona? It was pretty intense, and you had some narrow brushes with what could have turned out badly."

"You fared far worse than me. I do have nightmares occasionally, and I've developed a bit of claustrophobia. I do think about what happened and the vast reach of Coterie a lot. I started out as a sales rep for a pharmaceutical company and worked my way into a middle-management position. Even without my unintentional involvement in Arizona this hits a little close to home. The next victim could be someone I know."

"I didn't realize you had worked for a pharmaceutical company. Maybe that explains why Nick's been more supportive of my obsession from the start. Everyone else blew off the connections I was sure existed."

"Maybe, though I worked there before I met Nick. It was my first exposure to the food and drug manufacturing world. I've been primarily in food production ever since. I imagine Nick's support comes more from the fact that he trusts your instincts. He would have backed you no matter where I previously worked."

Devyn pondered what Morgan said about Nick's faith in her and thought about her obsession with the Risky Research investigation. To avoid losing another partner, she had tried to play by the rules at work since she and Nick started working together, and he had stuck with her. Now, the stakes were higher. Not only could she lose a partner if she crossed the line, but she feared losing Morgan, too.

"Delicious," Devyn stated while devouring the last slice, deciding it was time to lighten the topic of conversation.

"This is fun. Nick's not a huge fan of pizza and he's appalled when I eat raw cookie dough. He thinks it's uncivilized and dangerous."

"Yep, he seems to like a more refined dining experience," Devyn replied.

"Well, I, for one, can think of few finer things in life than pizza, cookie dough, and casual conversation with a good friend."

Devyn smiled. She wanted to be a good friend, but she was a little nervous treading into unfamiliar territory.

"I'm a little new to this 'girl's night' thing, but I suppose we should be talking about the wedding," Devyn said.

Morgan giggled. "We are keeping it very simple this time around. Everything is done since the big day is just around the corner."

"Is there anything I can do? I helped you pick out your dress, not that I know anything about fashion, but it seems like I should be doing more."

"Well, if I had a maid of honor, you'd be it. So, we'll call this my bachelorette party and you can consider your duty fulfilled."

TWELVE

Yesterday's call with Carson Grant caused Sofia to stay up most of the night thinking. She wondered how much more of herself she was willing to give to ensure Coterie's continued financial success and to please J.R. She shouldn't care about pleasing him. Allowing any man to hold so much power over her made her vulnerable and weak.

Sofia arrived at her foundation earlier than usual, hoping to reach her office before Trevor arrived. Sneaking around trying to avoid her staff was no way to live. Somehow, she had to regain some control over her life. But first things first. She needed to make it through a tough day. Today was Justine's funeral, and she had a few things to take care of before flying to Los Angeles.

The motion sensor lights flashed to life as she entered the lobby. The building she shared with a number of other companies was still blissfully quiet being so early in the morning. She entered the elevator and rode in silence to Buyer's Choice Foundation on the eighth floor.

Trevor's desk was empty, a situation she dreamed of making permanent. Strolling past, she twisted the knob on her door and entered. She flipped her lights on and unbuttoned her coat, her mind distracted by indecision about J.R. on a personal level and what to do about Carson's newfound confidence.

She wasn't sure if she could feel or hear breathing, but the sensation sent chills up her arms and a pulse of adrenaline surging through her veins. The jumble of thoughts instantly vanished and her focus returned. Rather than freeze and give away her knowledge of someone's presence, she finished removing her coat.

Spinning, she tossed her jacket in the direction she sensed a presence and jumped back several paces, placing her out of arms reach of the intruder. She raised her hands into an open-hand defensive posture.

As the person batted away her coat, she recognized her intruder, but she didn't relax her stance or lower her arms. "What are you doing hiding behind my door in the dark?" she demanded.

"I'm not hiding. I didn't expect you in so early. I was just investigating a noise. Remember, I'm here to protect you," Trevor replied.

"Bull! I don't need protecting when I'm not even here, and why would you investigate in the dark? I'll ask again, what are you doing in here?"

"My job."

"Which job? If you mean your sham of a job here, I'm your boss, and I demand to know what you're doing in my office in the dark so early in the morning."

"My other job for my other boss."

Sofia relaxed her fists and walked to her desk. She sat down, her hands in her lap. She suspected there was nothing to gain by pressing the issue any further and doubted he planned on hurting her or he would have already tried.

Her mind reeled trying to think of what he or J.R. could possibly want in her office. She shook her head and took a deep breath. She didn't want Trevor to realize how much he had shaken her.

"Since you're here, let's talk about this job. Did you take care of my flight arrangements for today?"

"J.R.'s sending his plane."

"Why?"

"He didn't say."

Talking to Trevor was exhausting and frustrating.

"What time do I need to leave for the airport?"

"Eight. He's sending a car. I'll notify you when it arrives."

Trevor turned and left, closing her door as he went. Sofia took several deep breaths and looked down at her trembling hands. She had been careless and it could have cost her. She wasn't sure why he unnerved her so, other than the fact that he had threatened to kill her during their first meeting, and she suspected he played some role in Justine's murder.

She needed to refocus, to regain the confidence and control she had spent years building. Distraction could be deadly. She couldn't afford to let down her guard around Trevor for even a moment. From here on out, she would always assume he was lurking somewhere nearby even if she couldn't see him.

Sofia paced to her window and looked out at the city slowly coming to life below. Nothing about this city felt like home or a place to really settle in. Home held mostly painful memories, except one. She picked up her phone and dialed a number she had kept in her head and close to her heart for twenty years. "Verda?"

"Is that you Sofia?"

"Yes. I hope I didn't wake you. I know it's early."

"Of course not. I may be getting old, but I still get up at the crack of dawn to exercise. The older we get, the harder we have to work to keep in shape."

"I assumed you'd be up, and I thought I'd take a

chance and call before my day got busy."

"It's so good to hear your voice. I can't remember the last time you called. I was worried something had happened to you. I prayed it was something good like you found a man and were too busy building a family of your own to remember a feeble old lady."

"Nothing could remove you from my memory, and I doubt you're feeble. I'm certain you could still send me to the mat anytime you chose."

The familiar cackle on the other end of the line felt like a balm to Sofia's tortured soul. Verda had saved her life, emotionally for sure, and maybe even physically. Even though she hadn't called the woman in years, Verda was never far from her mind.

As a child, Sofia wandered the streets every night after school, delaying going home as long as possible. Most nights, once she got home, she would hide in the crawl space under the house until her mother and the men she brought home either passed out or left the house for the bars or to score more drugs.

One afternoon as she wandered the streets after school, she had peeked into a community center and watched as Verda taught karate to teenagers. Verda's mission was to keep kids off the streets and refocus their potentially destructive energies into something more positive. Sofia was transfixed and came back every afternoon, getting a little bolder with each visit. Eventually, Verda coaxed her onto the mat, and that's when Sofia took up martial arts. More importantly, she had discovered someone who wanted nothing from her and asked no questions.

"I doubt that," Verda replied. "You possessed a special gift. All I had to do was to explain the purpose behind the various disciplines and show you the basic techniques and you would master each art."

"Are you still helping kids?"

"Yes, but now I have the kids play volleyball instead of teaching martial arts. At my age, I was worried one of the kids would unintentionally send me to the hospital. What are you doing now?"

"I built a successful business, which doesn't leave much time for a personal life, but I still go to the gym every day and practice everything you taught me."

"If you'd like to volunteer, I'm sure we could revive the martial arts program. It's a good outlet for angry and aggressive kids. It helps them channel their impulses into a more positive and disciplined form of release."

"I'm no longer in South Carolina, but I'd like to help. I remember how tough it was to secure funding and how important donations were in keeping the center running. You saved my life, and I'm now in a position to give back."

"You give me more credit than I deserve but thank you. As always, we're barely getting by down there, and every little bit helps."

Sofia thought back to the kind woman who had given her a little compassion and dignity for a couple hours five days a week. She never shared the truth of her childhood with anyone, including Verda, but the woman likely did save her life. Not only did she give her self-respect and confidence, but she taught her how to defend herself from the drugged-out losers her mother allowed in their home. On more than one occasion she had fended off lecherous advances, though it didn't take that much skill to send a stoned junkie to the floor for a long nap.

"No, Verda, you don't get enough credit. I can't

even imagine how many kids' lives you have touched over the years. When I think back to that time in my life, you are my only positive memory."

"I'm sorry for that, but I'm glad things have turned out well for you. I knew you were smart and tough, I just hoped you would direct your energies in the right direction, and it sounds like you have. I'm proud of you."

Sofia had to fight back the tears. Yes, she had built a successful business, but she had allowed over-ambition, anger, and the desire for revenge to lead her down a dangerous path. She doubted it was possible to turn back or change the direction she had chosen to follow. She had gone too far.

"Are you still at the same location?" Sofia asked.

"Unfortunately, yes. You think it was a dump when you were a kid, you should see it now. But it's not what's on the outside that matters. It's what's on the inside."

Sofia smiled. "Yes, you always used to tell us that. Thank you. After all these years, you still speak encouraging words."

For a moment, the line was silent. Sofia wasn't really sure why she had called. Maybe she just needed to hear a kind and caring voice.

"Did you ever find any happiness, Sofia?"

Sofia thought about the question. She was financially secure, and people respected her, but no one except for J.R. had ever tried to get close to her. She thought he cared about her, and she thought she might be in love with him. Now she wasn't sure where they stood. Apparently, he didn't trust her, but did he still harbor any feelings for her?

"I wish I could say yes, but I'd be lying, and you

always knew when I wasn't telling the truth. I'm content, and I've achieved my financial goals, but it's lonely at the top, as they say."

"Priorities, Sofia, priorities. We used to talk about that a lot as well as analyzing the consequences of one's decisions. It sounds like you need to take a step back and do a little soul searching. It's never too late."

Sofia feared it was too late for her, but she promised Verda she would try and disconnected the call.

By the time she finished talking to her childhood mentor and the only person she could ever remember getting a hug from, her focus returned. Sofia had already been thinking about her priorities and her future, but right now, she had more important issues to deal with like what Trevor was doing in her office.

Checking every nook and cranny for cameras or listening devices, she found nothing. Satisfied that the purpose of Trevor's intrusion wasn't to install surveillance equipment, she then opened every drawer in her desk and file cabinet. Nothing appeared missing or disturbed.

Everything about Buyer's Choice Foundation was legitimate on the surface. J.R. knew she held damaging information over the senator, which kept him obedient. She had refused to share her secret with him or anyone.

Was J.R. trying to find out what I have on the senator? If he could control the senator, my membership in Coterie might no longer be necessary. Maybe he was looking for some way to control me, or he's trying to verify my loyalty.

Sofia was too cautious to keep anything important at the office or at home. Anything worthwhile was kept in multiple locations to insure its survival. She not only rented a bank safe deposit box, but she leased a small storage unit outside the city. Her paranoia had paid off. If Trevor was searching for any dirt on her or the senator, the office was squeaky clean.

Her office door opened.

"So much for knocking," Sofia said as Trevor walked into her office.

"The car's here."

"Tell them I'll be right down. I have one quick thing to do before I leave."

Trevor left.

Sofia pulled up her address book on her computer. After finding the correct contact, she typed a quick message to her accountant and then dialed his number.

"I want to make a one hundred-thousand-dollar donation to a very worthy charitable organization. I've sent you all the details in an e-mail. Please cut the check as soon as possible and ensure that it's promptly delivered."

Sofia planned on going to Los Angeles for the funeral and returning to D.C. that night. With one last look around, she gathered up her handbag and left her office. She didn't even glance at Trevor as she strode past his desk and entered the elevator.

THIRTEEN

Devyn couldn't believe the change in her partner since his ex-wife reentered the picture. He was still wound tight but not to the same degree. Even though Nick had worked late teaching a women's self-defense class, before Morgan's arrival he would have still beat her to work by at least a half an hour. Today, she'd been the first to arrive, and it just didn't feel right.

She opened her e-mail and found the message she'd been awaiting. The answer, though, wasn't to her liking. The university would be happy to supply Aaron Truscott's school records once she submitted the attached form verifying her credentials and the authority under which the request was being made. Due to the often high-profile careers of its graduates, the university was required to follow strict protocols before releasing any information on past or present students. After they received the form, and if everything was in order, it would take three to five business days to process the request.

"Man, I hate bureaucracy," Devyn grumbled.

"Anything I can do?" Gordo asked.

Devyn looked up and saw the gangly computer tech holding a plate of cookies and standing next to her desk with a wide grin on his face.

"Probably, but I'd hate to get you into deep trouble by having you hack into a university records' system when I'm not sure it'll yield anything worthwhile. So, I'll follow their stupid rules and wait patiently for three to five business days for a response."

She couldn't interpret the look on his face. Was it a nervous smile or had she amused him with her "patient" comment?

"Take a seat. Nick's running late. What do you have there?" Devyn asked while nodding toward the plate in his hands.

"Mom baked cookies last night, and I thought you might like some."

"Are you trying to fatten me up with all these goodies?"

Gordo blushed. "No, that couldn't happen. I mean you're so skinny. Not too skinny, just right. You have a great shape. Not that I'm looking, it's just…"

Devyn held up her hand to stop him and put him out of his obvious angst. "It's OK, and thanks for the compliment and the cookies."

The young man relaxed. Nick was correct about Gordo. As much as his attention flattered her, she had to do something. "How old are you, Gordo?"

"Uh, twenty-four."

"You realize I've got about a decade on you, don't you?"

He shrugged his shoulders. "You don't look old."

"Thanks, again, but I sure do feel old with all these aches and pains. Have a cookie."

Gordo took a cookie, and for a moment, neither said a word.

"Can, can I ask you something?" he stuttered.

"Shoot."

"Rumor is you're seeing someone, but Gardner said you made him up."

Devyn took another bite and thought for a second.

"Between you and me, Gordo, I think so. I hope so. He's a great guy I've known for quite a while, but our jobs make a relationship difficult. He tried to take care of me last weekend, and I probably wasn't a very nice patient. That's why I say, 'I hope so.'"

The disappointed look on Gordo's face broke her heart. She wasn't sure what else she could say, so she said nothing.

After a few moments, he broke the silence. "Well I better get to the lab, or Fitz will be combing the halls looking for me. I'm sure your guy will stick around. If he can't handle a little uncooperative grumpiness when you're in so much pain he isn't worthy of you. If he bails, you know where to find me—I mean if you need anything."

"Thanks. You're a great guy and a huge asset to the Agency. Some young woman will be very lucky to have you."

Gordo's blush was endearing as he grinned and walked away. She hoped she had done the right thing setting the record straight, but she sure was going to miss the baked goods.

FOURTEEN

Sofia slid onto the soft leather seat of the black Town Car. She exchanged no words with the chauffer on the drive to the airstrip. Gathering her bag, she didn't wait for him to walk around and open her door. She was in no mood to thank anyone for anything, especially another one of J.R.'s employees.

When she stepped onto the plane, she stopped short. Her pulse raced at the mere sight of the stylishly dressed man standing in the aisle smiling. He probably didn't take most women's breath away, but he, unfortunately, had that effect on her. He was only an inch taller than her five feet nine inches, so when she was around him, she always wore low heels. His olive skin, dark hair, and dark eyes were attractive, but nondescript to those who didn't know the mind behind this complex and cunning man.

"Sofia, darling, you don't look pleased to see me."

"First of all, I didn't expect you, and second, you know I'm still furious about losing Justine and having Trevor forced on me. I don't like or trust him."

"Come, sit, have a glass of wine."

"It's eight thirty in the morning."

"A Bloody Mary, then?"

"No. What I want is Trevor out of my office and my life."

"We can talk about him later. I'm sure you're misunderstanding my intentions. I've simply come today to lend my support. I know losing your assistant was difficult for you, and I've missed you," he said as he closed the distance between them.

Sofia stood rigid, willing herself to be strong. She was too angry to just melt at his touch. He was like a dangerous drug. In her mind, she knew she must quit, but the addiction was almost too strong to fight.

J.R. took her bag and set it in the nearest seat. He ran a hand gently down her cheek and gazed into her eyes.

"So strong and so beautiful, yet so independent."

He gathered her into his arms and captured her lips in a demanding kiss. She fought the desire building inside her, refusing to relax her stiff posture. But after several seconds, her longing for him won out over her fear, anger, and resolve. She slid her arms up around his neck and returned the passion in his kiss.

Pulling her closer, she reveled in the warmth of his arms wrapped possessively around her. She couldn't deny it. She needed human contact as much as any woman, including her weak mother. Even more frightening, she craved this ruthless man, and she was powerless to resist him.

The thought of her mother gave her the strength to pull away. J.R. tilted her chin up and wiped the tear from her cheek with his thumb. The motion was tender and made her tremble, increasing her inner conflict. She doubted he would be capable of committing to one woman, and she had never shared anything with anyone. But could she live without him?

"What is it that makes you sad?"

"I don't want to care about you," she uttered, barely above a whisper.

He smiled. "I'm sorry that makes you sad because

it makes me very happy. I care about you too, Sofia, more than you can possibly imagine. You fear your feelings for me make you weak, but that's why I love you. You are the first woman I've ever had to work to obtain, and I knew that if you gave yourself to me it would be for reasons other than my fortune."

Sofia was so stunned by his admission of love, that she felt a bit lightheaded. She stumbled toward the two plush chairs and dropped into the one where she usually sat. She looked up at J.R., and the smile on his lips was genuine. "I think maybe I will have that Bloody Mary," she replied.

He snapped his fingers and an employee immediately responded. In minutes, the young man returned with two drinks, set them on the table between the chairs, and once again disappeared.

Sofia could detect J.R.'s eyes on her as she sipped the thick chilled drink. With distance between them, she sensed her sanity returning.

"You know I'm attracted to you and that I care for you, but I don't want this," Sofia stated.

"But we're so good together. I don't see the problem."

"You don't? There are many. Let me list them."

His smile remained as he nodded for her to continue.

"I doubt you can be in a monogamous relationship, and I don't share. I'm accustomed to being in charge of my life and my business, and you have manipulated both. And, if you had anything to do with Justine's death I can't get past that."

"I can and will be faithful to only you. I haven't been with another woman since the first time you walked into a meeting and put all the men in their place with merely a look. I was captivated and vowed to make you mine."

"That's a start, but what about the rest? I don't like being told to drop everything to do Coterie's bidding. You sent me to Arizona. When the young man I had mentored botched the job you made me destroy him. How could you ask that of me?"

J.R. reached over and took her hand. "What happened saddened me as well, but neither of us could have predicted how things would turn out in Arizona. I sent you because I trust you, and I had the utmost confidence that you would get the job done, which you did. I promise you, I will not place you into another dangerous situation. I was so angry at myself for putting you in such a precarious position that I couldn't face you when Max brought you to me. I hated myself for causing you so much pain. I'm probably not worthy of your love, but I can't live without you."

Sofia pulled her hand away from his. There were still too many unanswered questions for her anger to dissipate. She thought back to that day Max Markis had flown her from a remote airstrip in Arizona to J.R.'s private plane in Texas, and her disappointment with J.R.'s attitude when she arrived. Understanding why he avoided her that day helped but didn't resolve all the barriers still standing between them.

"If you trust me then why did you send Trevor to keep tabs on me, and what was he doing in my office before I was scheduled to arrive at work this morning?"

He threw his head back and laughed. "You think I sent Trevor to spy on you? No, darling, I sent him to protect you. I fear the FBI might be getting too close to your true identity. If they come for you Trevor's orders are to ensure your escape. He sweeps your office every morning for bugs. Do you realize how easy it would be for an agent to pose as a client and plant a listening device in your office? I also worry about this senator that you've been manipulating on our behalf. If you push him too far, he might send someone after you. And Coterie has made many enemies along the way. If you are ever tied to the organization, you will be in grave danger."

"I'm not buying it. I can take care of myself. I have since I was a child. Did Trevor tell you what happened the day we met?"

"Yes. You are fortunate that he knows how important you are to me. It may have seemed that you bested him, but do not underestimate him."

Sofia still wasn't sure she believed him. "But he told me you didn't trust me."

"I'm sure he was lashing out. Clearly, you two have gotten off on the wrong foot. It's difficult to keep someone of Trevor's skill tempered. Please try to get along until I'm more confident the danger has passed or until I can convince you to give up your business and join me."

She was at a loss for words. This was the first time J.R. had ever suggested she should give up her foundation to be with him. She thought her value to Coterie was in the connections her business fostered.

If she gave up her foundation and he no longer sent her to clean up messes, then she would be no better than her mother, totally dependent on a man for her survival. She couldn't let that happen or she had no doubt she would end up the same way—*dead*.

FIFTEEN

The short flight from Salt Lake City to Denver took a little over an hour. After picking up their rental car, Devyn and Nick headed west from the airport. Despite the heavy early morning traffic, she couldn't help but marvel at the beauty of the city framed by majestic mountains sporting caps of snow.

She could live here. It wasn't Wyoming, but surely it was close enough that maybe Gage could live here too. *Why does every thought always turn to Gage?*

"Are you paying attention? I think you just drove past our exit," Nick said.

"Sorry, I have a lot on my mind."

"Like a smooth-talking macho Wyoming sheriff?"

Devyn shot him the meanest look she could muster when he was dead on. "Do you want to drive?"

"No, I'm too busy recalculating the route. Looks like if you take the next exit we won't be too far off track."

Devyn and Nick drove the rest of the way to the Maggie Blair, Inc., headquarters in downtown Denver without incident. By the looks of the tall shimmering building at the center of the city, it was clear business had been going well for the company before the Giant Cactus Foods' bombshell rocked their world.

In the lobby Devyn and Nick showed their badges to the receptionist. She checked the schedule, made a brief call, and directed them to the elevator. She told them to go to the twelfth floor and someone would be waiting for them.

Devyn and Nick exited the elevator and found themselves in another elegantly decorated, yet smaller lobby with another reception desk. As promised, a young stylishly dressed woman strode toward them and smiled in greeting.

"Agents Nash and Melonis, I'm Ms. Blair's assistant. She is ready for you. Please follow me."

Devyn exchanged a look with Nick, not surprised by the efficiency. This empire was clearly run like a well-oiled machine, which verified what they had already ascertained from their background check of the business and of Margaret and Urban Blair.

They were ushered into a spacious and tastefully decorated office. An attractive middle-aged woman stood, rounded her desk, and met them halfway into her office.

"Hello, I'm Margaret Blair."

Devyn and Nick introduced themselves and took the offered chairs. Margaret returned to her desk and dismissed her assistant.

"You mentioned on the phone that you wanted to talk about Giant Cactus Foods. It's an Arizona Company, and I understand you're with the Salt Lake City FBI field office. What's the connection?" Margaret asked.

"We've been tracking a series of crimes that have occurred across the country over the past five years. We discovered a link between a victim in a Salt Lake case and a former employee of GCF. We contacted the Phoenix FBI field office, and through joint investigative efforts, we uncovered information that leads us to believe that the president of GCF had ties to a deadly criminal organization known as Coterie," Nick stated.

"Coterie, interesting name. I assume we're talking about a small group of like-minded individuals with a common mission and not a group of prairie dogs occupying a communal burrow," Margaret replied.

Devyn smiled. This woman was quick. "I'm afraid we're talking about ruthless killers and not a group of small fuzzy mammals."

"Well, I would do anything to bring those responsible for this disaster to justice. We've lost nearly forty percent of our business, and we anticipate lawsuits will start rolling in soon. Our stock has plummeted. It's too early to predict if we'll survive. Unfortunately, I'm not sure what I can do to help."

"How much interaction did you have with GCF and its president, Preston Hoyle?" Devyn asked.

"My husband and CEO of Maggie Blair, Urban, negotiated the contract. I never met or talked to Mr. Hoyle. I usually take a more active role in decisions that large, but when Urban presented the cost savings and health benefits of their miraculous sweetener, I guess I got greedy and sloppy. We've been with them for nearly two years, and until the news broke about the dangers of the sweetener, their products seemed too good to be true. And, clearly, they were."

"Is Mr. Blair in? We'd like to speak to him as well," Nick added.

Margaret picked up her phone and told her assistant to track down Urban and have him come to her office immediately.

"Ms. Blair, we understand that you've been a long-time generous contributor to Senator Carson Grant's campaigns." Devyn had probably just broken her promise to Conroy to proceed discretely.

"I have, and I plan to continue. He looks out for big business in a time where we are painted as villains. There's a fundraiser coming up in Washington, D.C., that Urban and I'll be attending. What does Senator Grant have to do with anything?"

Devyn noted the confusion etched on Margaret's face. "We've learned that he's been trying to block the merger of two smaller weight loss companies that are hoping to gain enough strength by pooling assets to compete with the top tier companies, which would include Maggie Blair, Inc."

"I'm aware of the potential merger. Word in the industry travels fast, but this is the first I've learned of Senator Grant trying to block it. I'm not surprised, and I'm sure he has his reasons. I can assure you I have not been in communication with him. Although I contribute generously to his campaigns, I doubt it's enough money to even suggest that large of a favor. Nor would I ask. In business, I believe in playing fair. I've gotten to where I am through hard work and good decisions and believe everyone should have that opportunity. I don't understand what this has to do with anything."

"Probably nothing. We're just trying to follow up on anyone who has any connection to GCF or any of the other related cases involving diet, pharmaceutical, nutrition, and fitness companies, no matter how peripheral," Devyn said.

"I see."

"While we're waiting for Mr. Blair, do any of these people look familiar to you?" Nick asked as he pulled up pictures of Aaron, Candace, Preston, and Janice on his cell phone.

"No. I'm very good at remembering faces, so I'm

certain I have never seen any of those people before."

~*~

Margaret's assistant wasn't at her desk. Urban paused outside his wife's door and listened. He could tell by the content of the conversation that she was talking to some sort of law enforcement about GCF. This did not bode well.

He peeked through the gap in the slightly opened door. He could see his wife studying something on the screen of a cell phone being held by a man. He debated about leaving, but he was certain Margaret's assistant would tell her that she had found him and delivered the message. Then he would have more explaining to do. Summoning up his courage, he pushed the door open and entered.

"Margaret, darling, what's so urgent that you had me pulled out of my meeting?" Urban stated as he strode into her office with as much confidence as he could muster.

"Urban, these are Agents Nash and Melonis from the FBI. They were involved in exposing the dangerous sweetener and all the tragedies surrounding the incident with GCF. They have a few questions I couldn't answer."

Nash and Melonis both stood and shook his hand. They remained standing since he did.

"We asked Ms. Blair about your company's interactions with GCF and its president, Preston Hoyle. She said all the contract negotiations were handled by you, so what can you tell us about the company and its president?" Nash asked.

"I only dealt with Mr. Hoyle a couple of times. I met with him to start the process and took a tour of the facility. It was impressive. We were both present when the contracts were signed, but most of the contract negotiations were handled by our respective legal teams. He seemed like a nice enough guy and appeared to be a shrewd business man. I pulled all the publicly available information I could on the company, and it had an impeccable record and impressive growth after the introduction of their new sweetener. I found no red flags."

"So you had never met Mr. Hoyle prior to that initial meeting?" Nash asked.

"Uh, no. That was the first time."

"We're generally very diligent with decisions of such magnitude as the manufacturer for our food products. Quality and safety are of the upmost importance. Urban received several glowing recommendations for GCF," Margaret added.

"Who offered those recommendations?" Nash asked.

"As I told my wife, I can't remember the names. We're trying to save the company. I haven't had time to focus on it. My secretary recently converted my old address book to an electronic contact list and cleaned out all the names I hadn't needed in the past couple of years so any contact information was likely destroyed."

"But you thought they were people you had met at the club and that one man was out of the country and the other deceased," Margaret added.

Urban nodded.

"What's the name of your club?" Nash queried.

Urban hesitated, and Margaret jumped in.

"I have the information right here. I was going to request the membership list in hopes of jogging Urban's memory, but I'm sure they'll be more willing to give it to you," Margaret said as she pulled a business card out of her drawer.

"Thank you," Nash replied.

Urban worked hard to keep a stunned expression from showing on his face.

Nash snapped a photo of the card with her phone and then handed it back to Margaret.

"One last thing, Mr. Blair," Melonis stated. "Do any of these people look familiar?"

Urban forced himself to keep a neutral expression, but one look at Nash's face told him, he'd let his surprise slip. He needed to cover, and quick. "That, of course, is Preston Hoyle, but I've never seen her or that other guy before in my life."

"I'm sorry we couldn't be of more help. Please keep me posted. Right now, I'm contemplating suing Mr. Hoyle's estate for our losses. People might see that as a little cold-hearted to go after the grieving widow, but someone must pay. I've given everything to this company. It's my life. I won't go down without a fight," Margaret said.

Urban rounded the desk and placed an arm around his wife's shoulders and pulled her closer. "If you don't need anything else I'll have someone show you out. As you can imagine, this has been a very difficult time for us, having everything we've worked so hard for jeopardized because of one man's greed. Maggie has been under a tremendous strain, so if you require anything further, please contact me directly," Urban stated as he looked down at his wife, making sure to let the agents see his love and adoration in his compassionate gaze.

"Thank you both for your time. If we learn anything, we'll be in touch, and if you think of anything else, please give me a call." Nash placed her card on Margaret's desk.

SIXTEEN

Sofia arrived at the office at her usual time, but already felt exhausted. She didn't get back home from Justine's funeral until well after midnight. True rest on the flight home had been impossible with all the thoughts running through her mind and with J.R. wanting to talk about their future. He was attentive, supportive, and convincing about everything except Justine's death. On that subject, she could describe him as nothing else but evasive.

The funeral was worse than she could have ever imagined. She had planned to say a few words to the family, sit in the back row of the church, and slip out as soon as possible. But the family had embraced her, insisted she sit with them, and ensured she didn't skip the gathering after the service.

She was surprised to learn how much the job had meant to her assistant and how vital any praise was to the young woman.

Between J.R.'s declaration of his love and vow to be faithful to her, the emotional strain of the funeral, her continued doubts about Justine's death, and the discomfort brought on by Trevor's presence, acid boiled in her stomach. Retrieving her purse from her bottom desk drawer, she fished around in the bottom until her fingers located the small round cylinder. She popped a couple antacids, leaned back in her office chair, closed her eyes, and tried unsuccessfully to clear her mind.

J.R.'s explanation about why Trevor was in her office didn't remove her concerns. The thought of the surly goon pawing through her domain every morning made her skin crawl and her anger surge. She owned very little with personal or sentimental significance, but what was hers was hers and no one else had the right to touch any of it without her permission.

Opening the shallow top desk drawer, she lifted the plastic tray organizing her pens and other office necessities and retrieved the age-yellowed envelope underneath. She lifted the flap and removed the small faded blue ribbon. *First Place – Inner City Karate Tournament.* She smiled as she smoothed her fingers over the stiff surface. The ribbon made her smile and reminded her to follow up with her accountant and make sure the check had been sent to Verda's community center.

Even though she doubted he found it, the thought of Trevor touching the only treasure from her youth made her fury once again simmer to the surface. She placed the ribbon back in the envelope and put it in her purse to take home. She only hoped he wasn't sweeping her condo as well.

As she returned her purse to its usual drawer, her door opened.

"A car will pick you up at your condo tonight at eight. J.R.'s called an emergency meeting, and we're convening at his compound in Miami for the weekend," Trevor stated and then left.

Sofia was conflicted about seeing J.R. again so soon with all her emotions in turmoil. More disconcerting, though, was the thought of traveling with Trevor. Her survival instincts always warned her to identify an escape route whenever she occupied the same space with him, but an airplane left few exit options once airborne, and that thought unsettled her.

When around J.R., she couldn't think rationally. She behaved like a woman in love, not a woman in firm control of her destiny. She couldn't afford to let down her guard for a moment. He told her not to underestimate Trevor, but never promised Trevor wouldn't carry out his treat to kill her.

Sofia was starting to believe J.R. truly cared for her. She doubted he would ever physically harm her, but she had no doubt he would break her heart, steal her independence, and she feared she was helpless to stop the inevitable conclusion.

SEVENTEEN

Devyn had never been more relieved for Friday to arrive. They had made some progress on the Risky Research case over the week, but the run-ins with Gardner seemed to be getting more frequent and more irritating. She shouldn't let him get under her skin, but he was difficult to ignore, especially when he tended to drag so many other agents into his childish games.

She wondered how different her working relationships could have been if it weren't for the confrontation with Gardner her first week on the job. He had hit on her, and she put him in his place in front of the entire floor. Maybe she could have handled the situation with more finesse, but not only was she not interested, but she could see the tan outline of his wedding band on his finger. He should have been embarrassed and ashamed by his behavior. Instead, he'd been an annoying jerk to her since.

Easing herself up from the sofa, Devyn shuffled into the kitchen, opened the freezer, and pulled out a pint of half-eaten chocolate peanut butter swirl ice cream. She grabbed a spoon and dug in as she leaned back against the kitchen counter, savoring each delicious bite.

She had nearly made it to the bottom when the phone rang. She groaned and thought about letting it ring, but if it was Gage, he was definitely worth an interruption in her ice cream eating. She answered.

"Hello."

"What are you up to?" His deep voice eased over her like a warm caress.

She smiled and placed the ice cream carton in the kitchen sink.

"I'd love to relay something exciting or noteworthy, but the truth of the matter is that I'm standing here in my kitchen eating ice cream out of the container. What are you doing?"

He laughed. The sound made her weak in the knees. She didn't know why he had that effect on her, but she finally decided to quit fighting it and enjoy exploring new territory.

"I'm sitting here on the front porch swing, drinking a beer, watching a beautiful Wyoming sunset sink toward the horizon and thinking the only thing in the world that could make it better was if you were here to share it with me."

Devyn couldn't speak. She was used to the way Gardner talked to her at work and the rude and insulting comments from the criminals she busted, but Gage was the first man to ever say kind and romantic things to her.

"You still there?"

"Yes. I was just trying to decide if you've had too many beers, because that's the sweetest thing any man has ever said to me."

"Nope, first one. How are you doing? Aches and pains getting any better?"

"I must be getting old. This isn't the first time I've cracked my ribs, but I don't remember it hurting so much or taking this long to heal."

"Wish I could have stayed longer to take care of you."

"I wish you could have stayed longer, too, but I had a few ideas in mind other than you making me soup."

There it was again, that rich laughter that made her want to crawl into his lap and run her fingers through his unruly hair and caress his freshly shaven face before capturing his lips in a seductive kiss.

"I have to confess. My intentions weren't quite so honorable when I started driving toward Utah, but when I saw how beaten up you were, I just wanted to make your pain go away."

Devyn thought she might cry. Plenty of co-workers and criminals wanted to cause her pain, but no one had ever wanted to take it away.

"What's wrong with those women up there? Any man who looks like you, has a job, and says stuff like that is major catch. I can't believe they're not knocking down your door."

"I let it leak to a couple of the dispatchers that I was involved with a super-tough smoking-hot FBI lady no woman would want to cross. I'm not sure if they actually broadcasted it over the radio or not, but pretty much everyone in town knows about us and my deputy has corroborated the story."

Devyn laughed but stopped short. "Don't make me laugh. It still hurts too much."

"Sorry. I won't keep you I just wanted to hear your voice."

"I'm glad you called. You always make a crappy day a whole lot better."

"Anything you want to talk about?"

Devyn wasn't sure if a man ever really wanted to listen to a woman's problems, even if he asked, but so far, he always meant what he said. She told him about her run-in with Gardner and having to let Gordo down easy. "Maybe you're making me soft, but I hated seeing the disappointment in Gordo's eyes and Gardner's comments are getting to me more than they used to. I've always been able to let it roll off, but I'm getting tired of all the nastiness. I could deck him or tell Conroy, but both of those options would probably do more harm than good. I'd get suspended if I beat him up, and the others would hate me if I tattled. Nick tries to run interference when he can, but I can't depend on him playing big brother all the time. So, I guess the only option is to keep taking his attitude."

"I could come beat him up for you. Conroy can't suspend me."

Devyn tried to stifle the giggles at the notion to avoid the shooting pain in her ribs. She had no doubt that if she wanted Gage to have a little man-to-man talk with Gardner he would. The knowledge that she had someone else besides Nick in her corner for a change, and the image of Gage towering over that weasel making him squirm, perked up her attitude considerably.

"Be careful what you offer. I may take you up on it one of these days."

"The offer stands."

They talked for a few more minutes. She hated to disconnect but didn't want to appear too needy.

"Well, I'll let you get back to your beer and sunset."

"Enjoy the rest of your ice cream."

The minute the line went dead, emptiness closed in. Devyn reached for the carton in the sink and lamented the liquid puddle of chocolate.

She definitely had it bad but didn't know what to

do about it. Maybe she would let Morgan take her shopping.

EIGHTEEN

Sofia arrived in Miami late. It was a miserable flight on J.R.'s private plane, having to share all the luxury with the brooding Trevor. Neither made any attempt to converse or to be civil to the other, but several times, Sofia caught him watching her. He didn't even try to pretend he hadn't been staring, and his actions sent chills up her spine.

Thankfully, it was a short flight. Sofia had never been so happy to be slapped with stifling hot humidity when the doors to the jet opened. They were picked up and driven to J.R.'s private compound, a short distance south of Miami.

She was relieved to be escorted to a private villa at the edge of the compound. Its second story bedroom provided stunning sea views over the top of the security wall surrounding the property. She opened the windows allowing the rhythmic sounds of the waves gently rolling in to reach her ears.

Slipping under the luxurious sheets, she tried to push all the discomforting thoughts from her mind concerning her growing fear of Trevor and her tumultuous emotions about J.R. She needed rest and hoped the time alone in this calming tropical setting would allow her to gather her thoughts and get her emotions under control before having to face J.R. and the rest of Coterie in the morning.

Despite all the turmoil of the past few days, Sofia

fell asleep immediately. She didn't wake up until the chirping birds outside penetrated through the fog in her brain and the sun shone brightly through the window of her seaside villa.

She rolled over, wishing she was on a vacation instead of being summoned to an emergency meeting. She needed to step back and examine her priorities like Verda suggested. Unfortunately, she never seemed to have that luxury.

As she got up and looked out the window at the ocean, she absorbed its beauty for the first time, and a sense of serenity washed over her. She inhaled the scents of the sea and the tropical vegetation cradling the villa and experienced a rare moment of peace. If she took J.R. up on his offer to leave D.C., this could be her life. But for how long? She wasn't sure which would come first, him tiring of her or her tiring of existing for the sole pleasure of someone else.

Resigned to the life she had created, she quickly showered, dressed, and made her way up a winding flower-lined path to the main house. She was pleased to see no sign of Trevor, though technically he was an employee of J.R., not a member of Coterie.

The rest of the Coterie members were seated around a grand table, clearly ready to begin and annoyed to be waiting on her. She didn't feel overly guilty. Being trapped at thirty thousand feet above the ground with someone who had already threatened to kill her hadn't been pleasant, so their wait wasn't a lot to ask of them.

Max Markis had a short flight from his apartment in New York. Urban Blair likely flew in from Denver the previous evening. Terrance Yeager resided in the Keys, only a couple hours south of J.R's estate, and always drove to these meetings.

Looking around the table, she couldn't help but question what she had gotten herself into. With the exception of J.R. and Max, these men were all weak and greedy. Urban and Terrance displayed the common desire for money and power, but neither possessed the determination or the stomach for the sacrifices that often took, the kind she had already made for the greater good of the group.

"Ah, there she is. Lovely as usual," J.R. said as he greeted her at the door.

He pulled her into his arms and kissed her deeply. When she stepped back, she could see the snide looks on the faces of her fellow members. She couldn't blame them.

J.R. pulled the French doors shut. "Grab something to eat and drink, and then we'll get down to business." He pointed to the elaborate spread of foods and beverages laid out on the sideboard.

As usual there appeared to be no staff running the estate, which she found odd. A home and grounds of this magnitude and so immaculately maintained, would require a sizeable crew, but she seldom saw anyone.

Sofia poured herself a cup of coffee and assembled a small plate of tropical fruits and freshly baked pastries. She purposely sat at the opposite end of the table from J.R. between Max and Terrance.

"Sleep well?" Max asked.

"Very well—all night and alone. Thank you for asking."

"Touchy this morning, aren't we?"

Sofia ignored his comment and sipped her coffee, waiting for J.R. to get the meeting underway. It was disconcerting to observe they were one member short. The empty chair reminded her how dangerous of a game they were all playing and that no one at the table could trust anyone, including the other members in attendance.

"It appears Sofia was correct. The mishaps in Wyoming and Utah have drawn the attention of the FBI, more specifically Agents Nash and Melonis of the Salt Lake Field Office. We were able to out-maneuver them for years with a little help from the inside, but I'm afraid we have lost that advantage and we must now make some adjustments."

"I say we all lay low for a while and distance ourselves from each other," Max stated.

"That may not be possible. Because Maggie Blair, Inc., purchased meals for its diet plan from Giant Cactus Foods, they've received a visit from the agents," J.R. replied.

"I warned everyone that doing business with each other was a risky and dumb move. We should always limit the ties linking us to each other to the highest extent possible," Max added.

"Agreed, but what's done is done," J.R. stated. "We need to focus now on containing the damage. Urban was questioned along with his wife. The agents were digging for ties between GCF and Maggie Blair. They asked about Margaret's contributions to Senator Grant's campaigns. What concerned me the most, though, was that they showed pictures of Aaron, Preston, and Sofia's two aliases to Margaret and Urban and asked if they recognized any of them."

"Sounds like Sofia better watch her back," Terrance stated.

"That's why I've sent Trevor to D.C., to protect her

at all cost."

"But who will protect us from her?" Terrance mumbled.

Sofia heard, but either J.R. didn't or he chose to ignore the comment. She was starting to understand J.R.'s concern for her safety. After what happened to Preston Hoyle in Arizona, she couldn't rule out a preemptive strike from her peers. Add the senator and the FBI to the mix, and she felt the walls closing in on her.

"Urban didn't think they had anything concrete, except for the photos of Sofia's aliases, Candice Rogers and Janice Green, and were primarily on a fishing expedition. His wife gave them some information that will probably keep them busy for a while doing pointless background checks on everyone at his country club. Even though the connection between his wife and Senator Grant has nothing to do with Coterie, I think Sofia should tighten the collar on the senator. We've probably gone to that well too many times, so for now we need to make sure he doesn't lead the FBI to Sofia. Do you require assistance or can you assure the senator's silence and continued cooperation?"

Nausea churned in the pit of Sofia's stomach. There was no point in delaying the inevitable any longer. She held the cards. Now she had to play them. She'd have to relive a part of her life she had spent decades trying to forget. She lifted her eyes from the table and met J.R.'s gaze.

"I can control the senator."

"I'd love to know what she has on that pathetic excuse for a human being," Max stated. "It must be good for her to have kept that weasel under her thumb for so long."

"You talk tough about Carson Grant here, but you've probably already R.S.V.P.'d for his fundraiser," Terrance added.

"Sure did. He throws a heck of a party and everyone who's anyone in business will be there, and I'm someone in business. It would look odd if I didn't show. Did you even get an invite?"

"Of course, I did," Terrance replied. "My media company is largely responsible for many of them being elected to office."

"And?" Max asked.

"Yep, I'm going, too. I've produced his and half of the Senate's campaign ads and printed materials. I have no intention of missing this opportunity to keep those ties strong going into another election cycle."

"I suppose you're planning on attending as well, Urban?" J.R. asked.

"Are you kidding? Margaret lives for those types of events. Of course we're going."

"Talk her out of it. I think we're well enough represented, and it's always risky to put too many of us in the same room together, especially right now. If they happen to discover our membership it would be a simple exercise to round us up."

Sofia didn't mention that she had received an invite as well since she hadn't decided if she planned to attend. Her gut told her to stay away, but there were a number of reasons to scope it out.

"But it's so important to Margaret. Since it's my fault we got into bed with GCF in the first place and may lose the company as a result, I don't want to deprive her of this little joy. Besides it might take her mind off of finding a scapegoat," Urban said.

"Scapegoat?" J.R. asked.

"Yes, she's determined to find someone to blame. She's mentioned suing Preston's estate, and she keeps hounding me for the names of those who recommended GCF. The only person who recommended GCF to me is Preston, and he's dead. She agreed to talk to the FBI without consulting me, wanting to find out if the authorities possessed any information she could use to make someone pay for our loss."

Sofia said nothing but feared Urban had said too much. Everyone knew he worshipped his wife, but that wouldn't matter to J.R. if he thought she had become a dangerous liability.

"A lawsuit against Preston's estate wouldn't be good for any of us. Having opposing lawyers digging too deeply may expose ties we need to keep hidden. Preston clearly wasn't as shrewd as I originally thought. Sofia swept his office for any incriminating evidence while she was there, but we have no way of knowing if he kept records hidden elsewhere."

"What do I do?" Urban asked.

"It sounds like you're incapable of controlling your wife. I suppose there's nothing you can do, so forget about it," J.R. replied.

"Thanks. I just don't want to upset her anymore right now. The possibility of losing our company has been very difficult for her."

Sofia couldn't believe Urban's naivety. Could he possibly think J.R. would cave so easily? If J.R. didn't want Margaret at the fundraiser, the woman would not attend. Sofia only hoped J.R. would keep his word, and she would not be sent to prevent Margaret from attending the event or from talking to the FBI.

Her gaze landed on Preston's empty chair. He had

willingly joined Coterie and had been aware that drastic measures were often required in order to achieve the desired results or to silence those who could destroy them all. Margaret, on the other hand, was faultless except for her decision to marry Urban.

NINETEEN

Devyn was more chipper than usual for a Monday morning. Her body was finally on the mend. She could now laugh or sneeze without whimpering like a frightened puppy. Despite the progress though, her ribs still required more time before she'd be one hundred percent healed, so she would continue to follow the doctor's orders and take it slow.

For the third weekend in a row, she had lounged around the house doing nothing. The inactivity nearly drove her crazy, making her anxious to get into the office and dig back into the Risky Research investigation. She could sense they were getting very close to uncovering the identity of some of the players.

The elevator doors opened. Not spying Gardner anywhere, she hustled across the room as quickly as possible. When she reached her desk, she found a cinnamon roll covered with plastic wrap. She picked up the small note.

Even if you don't want to date me, I still think you're the best agent here (don't tell Nick). Friends?

As soon as her computer came to life Devyn pulled up Gordo's e-mail address. *Friends for sure. Thanks!* Clicking the send icon on her short e-mail, she looked up with a smile still on her lips to see Nick approach their desks.

"If that's supposed to be from a secret admirer, he's not very good at the game. I thought you talked with Gordo and set the poor guy straight."

"I did. He's just letting me know there are no hard feelings. In fact, if I were ten years younger I might have given him a shot. Even though he's not my usual type, the kid's put most of these so-called men around here to shame, present company excluded."

"But he can't compete with the sheriff, huh?"

"You're the only one around here that's met Gage. I'm right, aren't I? He's a great guy?"

Nick chuckled. "He seems like a good enough guy and a competent sheriff. Next time he comes to town for a visit we can all do dinner. I'm sure Morgan would be happy to provide a thorough assessment of his various assets."

"Speaking of Morgan, I need to check if she's free to go shopping next weekend. She promised to help me find a few new items to add to my wardrobe that Gage will find impossible to resist."

"Too much information. Let's get to work."

"Unlike you, I have been working. Late Friday night, I finished going through the membership list we got from Urban Blair's country club. I couldn't find anything that would tie anyone at the club to GCF enough to offer up a recommendation, and everyone on the list is alive and in the country."

"In other words, another dead end?"

Devyn nodded, but she didn't think it was a totally wasted effort. She not only crossed one task off her list, but the lack of any viable option and no deceased or out-of-the-country members added to her suspicion that Urban might be holding out on them.

Looking up, Devyn spotted the young female officer approaching their desks. "Oh, great." She'd been chasing after Nick for far too long, without him giving her any encouragement.

"Hi, Nick. Got a priority envelope and thought I'd bring it up instead of calling. You're always so busy solving important cases."

Devyn rolled her eyes. When would this gal give up? Nick was the only agent on the floor who got his priority mail hand delivered, and she found this woman's obsession with Nick annoying. After Devyn denied her request to fix her up with Nick, the woman had been rude to her ever since. Glancing over at the express envelope in the woman's hand, Devyn saw that it was her name on the label, not Nick's.

"Thanks," Devyn said as she snatched it from her hand. "I hope it's Nick and Morgan's wedding gift that I ordered. Oh, guess not, it's too small."

The young officer's mouth dropped open and she stared at Nick for an uncomfortable moment. "Is that true, or is she just being nasty as usual?"

"It's true. Thanks for bringing up the envelope."

Without responding, the woman shot Devyn a hateful glare and stomped off.

"Was that necessary?" Nick asked.

"I'd bet Morgan would think so. That woman's been throwing herself at you for a year now. I think it's time to burst her little bubble."

"Maybe, but I'm sure there was a kinder way to do it."

Devyn shrugged her shoulders. "Probably but fighting off all the hopeful women around here has been exhausting these past couple years. Besides, I've been waiting for this and was in no mood to watch her flirt with you while this investigation is going nowhere. It's the information I requested from the university Aaron attended."

Ripping open the envelope, Devyn retrieved the stack of papers and quickly skimmed through them.

"You're not going to believe who wrote a letter of recommendation to get Aaron accepted. Come on. Conroy has got to hear this, too."

TWENTY

Urban left Miami with a sick feeling. Had he said too much? He didn't want J.R. to think Margaret was a threat to Coterie. She didn't know anything about the organization or Urban's involvement with the group. She was simply angry and looking for someone to blame for her company's current crisis.

There was nothing she could tell the FBI that would expose any of them, but the fact that she was willing to talk to Agents Nash and Melonis made everyone, including him, very nervous. Not only did he need to figure out a way to keep her from talking to the authorities, now his peers expected him to dissuade her from going to Senator Grant's fundraiser. He hated those things and would gladly pass, but she lived for those kinds of social events and after everything she had been through in the past weeks, he couldn't deny her.

"Good news, darling," he said as he walked into Margaret's office. "I think we've halted the mass membership exodus. We only lost a half of a percent this weekend."

"That's progress, but clearly the goal is no net loss and some sign the tide is turning back in our favor."

"We'll get there. As soon as the new meals and desserts come online and the news fades, I'm sure we'll start seeing those numbers crawl back up. We've completely reworked the menu offerings so old members aren't reminded of the catastrophe. We're going to market the revamped meal plans as a new and improved line with innovative choices for the discerning pallet."

"I wish I shared your optimism. I guess a weekend of golf in Florida did help your attitude."

"It did. I understand you were uncomfortable leaving the company completely unattended, even for a weekend, but it would have been much more enjoyable with you there."

He had asked her to go along, confident she wouldn't with the company in crisis. Besides, she hated golf and had very little use for Florida. Luckily, his invitation hadn't backfired. If she had agreed to accompany him, he would have actually had to play golf, which he wasn't all that fond of either, and skip the emergency Coterie meeting. That would not have set well with J.R. since Margaret was partially the reason for the meeting in the first place.

"Someone needed to stay behind and be the responsible adult," she mumbled as she looked back down at the report she was reading.

"I'm sorry. I shouldn't have gone away either, but we've both been under a tremendous amount of stress ever since the collapse of GCF. If we can't get away together, why don't you take the company jet to Santa Fe this weekend and spend a few days at that spa you love so much. A couple of massages, a facial, a body wrap, some yoga and meditation, and a soak, and you'll feel rejuvenated."

"I can't do that. I doubt we're done putting out all of the spot-fires that keep popping up at every turn."

"Nothing that I can't handle over the weekend when the markets are closed and most of the employees, including the legal team, are off. We have the best public relations staff in the business, and they're handling the fallout. Besides, I can call if something comes up that requires your attention."

"I could use a break. I doubt I've slept for more than a few hours at a time since the GCF news broke. My eyes are strained, my muscles are tight, and I can't stop worrying."

Urban walked around her desk and rolled her chair backward, spinning it around until she faced him. Grasping her hands, he eased her out of her chair and into his embrace. He held her close, gently rubbing his hand up and down her back until the tension eased from her rigid body.

"Let me take more of the burden. Enjoy a weekend of pampering. When you get back, I want you to lean more on me. You can handle those things that need your personal touch, and I can take care of the rest. Let me deal with the authorities and the lawyers and all the other ugliness involved in cleaning up this mess. You can focus on rebuilding. It was your creative vision that built this company, and it will be your innovative ideas that return it to its rightful place at the top of the industry."

She leaned her head against his shoulder and said nothing. Holding her in his arms made him hope that he could save the company and save his marriage. She would always be his world, and everything he did revolved around her happiness.

After a few minutes, he gently leaned her back, just enough so he could look into her eyes. "Well?"

"You're probably right. It would do me good but letting go isn't easy for me."

"Promise me you'll at least think about it."

"I will, but right now, I'm late for a meeting."

She stepped out of his arms and grabbed her tablet. She gave him a quick peck on the cheek and hustled out the door, leaving him standing alone in her vast office, wondering if he had done the right thing by encouraging her to leave.

TWENTY-ONE

Devyn tapped gently on Special Agent in Charge Gerald Conroy's door and poked her head inside.

"Got a minute, boss? I received some information you need to hear."

Conroy waved her in. "What do you have?"

"I requested Aaron Truscott's records from the university he reportedly attended about four years after Aaron Holmes dropped off the face the earth. You are never going to believe this," Devyn stated almost too excited to talk.

"Then you better just spit it out, and I'll decide."

"The recommendation letter that got Aaron accepted into such a prestigious school came from none other than Senator Carson Grant," she said as she slapped the photocopied letter down on Conroy's desk in front of him.

She looked over at Nick, enjoying the stunned look on his face. She fidgeted anxiously while waiting for Conroy to absorb the information in the letter. It would be impossible for anyone, including Conroy, to deny or ignore all the ties linking the Senator to Coterie.

"Sit," he said as he picked up his phone and dialed the number in the letterhead. He placed the phone on speaker, so she and Nick could listen to both sides of the conversation.

"Senator Grant's Office, how may I help you?" asked the eager-sounding young female who answered the phone.

"This is Special Agent in Charge, Gerald Conroy, with the FBI's Salt Lake Field Office. I would like to speak to Senator Grant."

"He's unavailable right now. May I ask to what this pertains, and someone will get back to you shortly?"

"I need to ask him some questions about a college recommendation letter he wrote for a person of interest."

"Um, can you hold for a moment?"

Before he could answer the line filled with loud classical music. After several minutes, a much more mature male voice came over the line, replacing the annoying tunes.

"This is Adam, Senator Grant's senior aid. The senator is unavailable, but if you'll give me the name of the person on the recommendation and the approximate date, I can pull the file for the senator. We send out dozens of recommendation letters each year for constituents' children trying to get into military academies, prestigious schools, and the like. There's no way he can recall them all without a little background."

Resigned that the call would produce no results, Conroy gave the man Aaron Truscott's name and the date on the letter. He hung up the phone. "I don't expect a call back today, but I'll let you know when I hear something. The senator better provide a good explanation, or I may let Devyn go to D.C. and keep an eye on him after all."

"It would be my pleasure, sir. Just say the word and I'm on the next plane."

"I'm sure you would enjoy rattling the senator's

cage in person, but we need to give him a chance to explain. I can't fathom what he could possible say to dampen my suspicions that he's involved with this Coterie mess in some capacity, but we'll give him the benefit of the doubt for now."

"But, sir."

Conroy held up his hand. "I know you're impatient, but let's tread lightly so we're not ordered to stand down again."

"I assume the tread of my boot on his face isn't light enough," Devyn mumbled as she and Nick shuffled out the door.

TWENTY-TWO

Sofia dug through her purse to retrieve her ringing pre-paid cell. She almost missed the unfamiliar ring tone of the seldom-used phone. The only two people who possessed the number were J.R. and Carson Grant. Neither would be calling if it wasn't important.

"Yes," she said as she quietly went to her office door and locked it to prevent Trevor from barging in.

"The FBI in Salt Lake City called yesterday about a letter of recommendation for admission into an Ivy League School for an Aaron Truscott. I made that recommendation about seven years ago. Is this the same guy who died in Phoenix amid the Giant Cactus Foods' collapse that's been all over the news for the past couple of weeks?"

"It is."

There was a long pause. Sofia had forgotten about the recommendation letter she demanded Carson sign for Aaron all those years ago. When Aaron died, she should have guessed that the authorities would dig far enough into his past to uncover his college records. This information did not bode well for her.

"I feared one of your 'little favors' would come back to haunt me someday. What on earth am I supposed to tell the authorities?"

"Play stupid. You're good at that. What kind of records do you keep on this sort of thing?"

"All I can find is a copy of the letter, and

fortunately, my staff isn't aware it's in my possession. They're still digging through files looking for it. There was nothing jotted on the letter stating where the request came from. Usually I put a note on each letter explaining why we sent the recommendation, for instance if the parent is politically connected or makes a very large donation. The lack of documentation is what reminded me the request had come from you."

Sofia tried to sound calm, but this was bad. If Carson mentioned her name it would be all over. Her aliases had never been tied to her true identity, but if they learned her real name and checked her photo or came for a visit, she doubted her covers would hold under that kind of scrutiny. She needed to persuade him to weave the most convincing coverup story of his career.

"I'm done doing your dirty work, and I most certainly won't lie to the FBI for you. I'm going to tell them the truth that the request came from one of the most influential lobbying firms in the city, and you can deal with them when they show up at your door."

"I wouldn't do that if I were you. It would destroy your family."

"How would telling the truth and sending the hounds your way destroy me or my family? I don't know this Aaron guy, and I've never met him. I simply did a favor for you based on your assurance this young man had what it took to go to one of the best schools in the nation and that a helping hand from a concerned member of Congress would turn his life around. If I don't call the FBI back soon, they'll think I'm purposely stalling."

"I need to show you something before you make that call. Where can we meet?"

Carson paused. Sofia wondered if he was debating whether or not to meet her or if he was trying to think of a safe place where neither would be recognized.

"Well, I do keep a small apartment in the city that I maintain for when I need to get away and unwind."

Sofia shook her head in disgust. *Pig, just like his old man.*

They decided on a time later in the afternoon. She jotted down the address and slid it into her front pocket. Disconnecting the call, she stowed the phone in the bottom of her purse. The call shook her usual confidence and she needed to regroup before meeting him. The afternoon was going to dredge up all the ugliness of her past, and it would require all her strength to get through the rest of the day.

Rising, she unlocked her door, not wanting to make Trevor suspicious if he tried the knob. She returned to her desk and dropped into her chair, staring at her blank computer screen. After her weekend meeting with Coterie, she feared she'd have to play her last card, but she didn't think it would happen so soon.

Her mind wandered back to that horrible day when she had witnessed the crime. She hadn't cried nor felt anything but anger. She delayed calling 9-1-1 until the next morning, certain that the moment she did she would be relegated to a life of foster homes until she turned eighteen. The authorities ruled her mother's death an accident. She knew differently and could have proved it, but what would it have changed, except to prolong her misery?

She needed to run a few errands before the meeting, and she could use some time alone to gather

her thoughts and rehearse how the meeting should play out. She took a deep breath and gathered her purse and her courage. When she stepped out of her office, Trevor looked up.

"J.R. wanted the senator controlled. I'm taking care of it today. Stay here and reschedule all my afternoon appointments. Do your job here for a change, and don't follow me or you may destroy my plan. If he sees my goon, he'll likely bolt."

Sofia didn't give Trevor a chance to respond as she punched the down arrow on the elevator. The elevator arrived and the doors opened, exposing her next client.

"I'm very sorry, Mr. Tucker, but an emergency has come up I must deal with immediately. Mr. Montoya will reschedule our meeting."

Mr. Tucker's timing couldn't have been better. With Trevor occupied rescheduling the appointment she would be able to get out of the building without him trying to follow her.

Sofia pressed the button for the ground floor and closed her eyes. She had prayed this day would never come. Now that it had, she hoped she was strong enough to call Carson's bluff.

TWENTY-THREE

"I can't believe Senator Grant has blown off Conroy this long. It's been nearly twenty-four hours," Devyn said as she and Nick took a break from the list of cold calls they were making to pharmaceutical and medical research and testing companies.

"Makes you wonder if he's scrambling to cover his tracks or if he's playing the usual political power games with the FBI," Nick replied.

"Probably a little of both. Even if he had nothing to hide he'd still put off calling Conroy back as long as he can."

"I wish we could uncover some new piece of evidence that ties all of the loose ends together. So far, all these calls have been a major waste of time. Since we learned how Aaron got into college, now we need to figure out what he was doing between the time that Aaron Holmes disappeared and Aaron Truscott enrolled in school and from the time he graduated and went to work for Giant Cactus Foods," Nick stated.

The din in the large shared work space silenced, interrupting their conversation.

Devyn caught Morgan's attention and waved to her as she made her way toward her and Nick.

"No wonder you don't like Morgan coming down here. Gardner and his pack of dogs are practically panting as they're leering at your fiancée."

Nick didn't answer, but Devyn could tell by his

body language that he was contemplating giving Gardner another black eye. She chuckled as Nick stood, smiled at Morgan as she approached, and pulled her into his arms for a very long and inappropriate work-place kiss. Nick wasn't much on public displays of affection, so it was entertaining to watch him get so territorial over Morgan.

When he stepped back, Devyn noticed that he stood behind Morgan, blocking the view of her backside from Gardner and the rest of the men, who were slowly returning to their previous conversations.

"Um, hello to you, too, Nick and Devyn," Morgan stated, clearly as surprised as Devyn by Nick's behavior.

Devyn smiled, "So what brings you down here in the middle of the day?"

"I was doing some shopping and discovered this great little bakery not too far from here. Nick said you let poor Gordo down, so I thought you might be having goodie withdrawals. These brownies probably aren't as tasty as the ones Gordo's mom makes, but I thought they'd be better than nothing if you're desperate."

Devyn took the bag from Morgan's hand and peeked inside. A slow smile spread across her lips.

"If I knew friends did nice stuff like this, maybe I would have gotten one sooner," Devyn said, taking a frosted square out of the bag and sinking her teeth into the soft chocolaty square.

"These are to die for. Maybe Gordo's mom works there," Devyn stated as she held the bag out to Nick and Morgan.

Nick didn't even acknowledge the offer, and Devyn figured he was stewing too much to eat.

"Sorry about Nick's bad manners. Take a seat."

Once Morgan sat down, Nick returned to his chair, still scowling.

"That expression doesn't match the welcome you just gave me," Morgan teased.

"Sorry," Nick replied. "Someone needs to teach a few of those guys some manners. It's bad enough the way Gardner treats Devyn, but you're a civilian and they should show you a little more respect."

"When you got off the elevator all the men stopped chatting and lined the walkway like it was a parade route. It was pretty obvious they were ogling you, kind of like Nick's kiss was a clear attempt to mark his territory," Devyn offered.

"How sweet," Morgan said. "I'm glad I'm worth fighting for this time."

"Devyn, you're not helping. If we hope to ever bring down Coterie, we'd better get back to work."

"Speaking of work, maybe Morgan can help. Do you have any idea what Aaron did before showing up as an over-educated executive assistant for you at GCF?"

"I was provided his resume when I started, and I questioned Preston on his excessive qualifications. It said he worked for a lobbying firm in D.C. and a pharmaceutical company before that, but I can't remember the names of the companies or where the pharmaceutical company was located. I suppose all the information might be erroneous since we learned he wasn't who he claimed to be. If my old office hasn't been cleaned out, Aaron's resume would have been in the file drawer marked personnel files."

"I'll give Tanner a call and have him check the evidence log for your personnel files," Devyn replied.

"I'd better get going before the groceries in the car get too warm."

"I'll walk you out," Nick stated.

Devyn watched as they headed across the room toward the elevator. Every man, including Gardner, diverted their eyes as they passed but looked up to leer at Morgan once Nick could no longer witness them. Normally, Devyn would have been disgusted by their caveman behavior, but Nick's irritated response was too good to watch.

TWENTY-FOUR

After leaving her office Sofia went to her bank and retrieved a flash drive from her safe deposit box. Certain that Trevor hadn't slipped out and attempted to follow her, she made her way to the nearest Metro stop and boarded the train, clutching the flash drive in her hand.

Sofia hadn't looked at its contents since she had copied the file from a compact disc to a flash drive years ago, always vigilant to keep up to date on the current data storage media for easy retrieval.

She vowed to never look at the video again. Each time she watched it, she experienced less anger and more guilt. Maybe she could have stopped the tragedy, but at a minimum, she should have called for an ambulance even though it wouldn't have changed the outcome.

Despite the conflicting emotions ripping at her conscience, there was no point in delaying the inevitable any longer. The time had come to share her darkest most painful secret with Carson.

Holding the drive made memories of the night that eventually sealed her fate reel through her mind like a very bad low-budget movie. As with most evenings she had stayed at Verda's gym until it closed to delay going home as long as possible.

The sun was setting as she let herself in the back door leading into the kitchen of the small run-down house she shared with her mother. The television droned on in the next room as it did every night. She never checked in with her mother, not knowing how sober she might be or if she would be on a high or in a state of extreme depression. Sofia had no patience or sympathy for her mother's roller-coaster emotions.

Quietly and without turning on any lights so as not to announce her presence, Sofia made herself a peanut butter and grape jelly sandwich as she did most evenings. She sat at the small aluminum-frame, Formica-top table in one of their only two yellow and orange vinyl chairs, both patched with ample amounts of silver tape. She ate in silence, fearing who, besides her mother, might be in the house.

When the doorbell rang she quickly finished her sandwich so that she could hide in the crawl space if necessary as she often did when her mother entertained visitors. She listened as her mother shuffled to the door. When her mother greeted the new arrival, Sofia had relaxed.

George never paid her any attention, and though he was the ultimate root of their predicament, he was paying the rent on the dump and the utilities, so she tolerated his presence. He even brought her neat presents as bribes to keep her quiet and out of the way, usually some sort of new technology. The most impactful was the camera phone that hadn't even hit the open market yet, so she couldn't make calls, but could take videos.

"Is Sofia home?" he asked her mother.

"Not yet. We have the place all to ourselves," her mother purred.

Her mother's attempts at seductiveness made Sofia sick. Her mother had clearly been a remarkable beauty at one time, but age and drugs had taken a toll on the woman, making her overtures seem pathetic rather than sexy.

Sofia had pretty much been taking care of herself since she could remember. By the age of fifteen, she had heard and seen more unpleasantness than most people twice her age and much more than any child should ever have to witness.

Her education into the darker side of life had taught her to assess people, and she realized this man was important, but not overtly dangerous. She resented the squalor they lived in because of him. Someday he would pay. She just wasn't sure when or how, but she always recorded his visits in case he might provide her with something she could use against him one day.

The train slowed, jolting Sofia back to the present. She looked up and recognized her stop. She pushed the unpleasant remembrances out of her mind and exited the train. She walked three blocks and stopped. Pulling the slip of paper out of her pocket, she compared the number on the building with that scrawled on the note. This was the address.

She glanced at her watch. She had arrived precisely on time for her meeting. The desire to turn around and leave tugged at her, but she squared her shoulders and slowly ascended the steps leading to the front door.

The building wasn't as nice as she would have expected for a senator's play house, but then again, he probably wanted to avoid a building with a doorman or security cameras. Sofia shunned the ancient looking elevator and took the stairs to the third floor. She paused outside the door for only a moment, resigned to the fact that delaying was pointless.

Her goal was no longer to simply keep him on a tight rein to do her bidding in furtherance of Coterie's mission. With the FBI looking into Aaron, she feared her survival and freedom might depend on her ability to control the senator.

She took a deep breath and knocked. The door opened.

"Let's make this quick. I'm a busy man."

Sofia strode into a room that was much nicer on the inside than she would have thought judging by the address and the building's exterior. She set her purse on the table and pulled out her tablet. Powering it up, she inserted the thumb drive into the port. Propping the tablet up on the counter, she tapped the play arrow on the video and stepped back to allow the senator an unobstructed view.

"I brought you something special," Senator George Grant said.

"Oh, Senator Grant, you shouldn't have."

He pulled a bag out of his pocket containing what Sofia new from the autopsy report to be cocaine. "I assume you have everything you need to prep it?"

Her mother greedily grabbed her supplies off of the end table and set to work. George watched, not touching anything. Sofia looked away as her mother stuck the needle into her own arm without hesitation.

Sofia paced to the other side of the room, not wanting to relive the vulgar conversation that ensued as her mother tried to seduce the senator while getting less and less coherent. Sofia studied Carson Grant as he stared transfixed at the grainy video. She couldn't read his body language. He stood rigid, arms crossed, eyes focused on the small screen.

"Ready for another shot?" George asked.

Her mother's response was unintelligible. She took several unsteady steps toward the couch and collapsed onto the stained cushions. George pulled a pair of latex gloves out of his pocket, slid them on, and picked up the syringe. He filled it and stuck the needle in her mother's limp arm. He repeated the process two more times.

"I've seen enough," Carson said as he turned from the screen.

Sofia retrieved her tablet, stopped the video, and removed the flash drive.

"Would you like a copy? I made multiple copies," she said as she extended the flash drive toward him on her upturned palm.

He turned away without taking the offered item and walked to the window. He said nothing as he stared out the pane, running his fingers through his hair.

"I want you to tell the FBI you don't remember where the request for the recommendation letter came from. It was nearly seven years ago, and you get a lot of requests. You can't find any records to support the letter. Your staff prepares all of your correspondence, which I assume is true, and you sign, trusting all requests have been vetted. If you lead the FBI to me this video goes to the police and the media."

Sofia wasn't surprised by the quiet introspection. She suspected he was still processing the contents of the damaging recording he had just viewed, trying to come up with an explanation to refute what the video clearly documented—his father committing murder. She waited patiently for his answer, and finally he turned toward her.

"Why haven't you used this before now? You could have demanded so much more than a few political favors," he asked in a beaten-down tone she had never heard from him before.

"Because I didn't need to. I don't want or need your money, and it used to be so simple to attain your help to make my lobbying job easier. One of my ex-employees got into a lot of trouble, and he's now dead. I will not let you or him drag me down, too."

"I'll do my best to convince the FBI that I have no idea who the request came from. Occasionally, we get requests from students themselves with sob stories on how getting into this or that college could change their life, maybe this was one of those."

"Now you're thinking. Just make sure you give the performance of your life. If I go down I'm taking the whole family with me, dear brother."

TWENTY-FIVE

Urban watched his wife as she opened the elegant lunch menu. The act was more habit than necessity since she always ordered the same salad at this restaurant. After a quick scan of the offerings, she placed the menu to the side and looked impatiently over her reading glasses at him.

"Have you thought about getting away?" Urban asked.

"I've decided to take your suggestion and go to the spa in Santa Fe for the weekend. I'll ask my assistant to make the arrangements."

"I'm pleased to hear that. You've been working too hard, and you deserve a break. I can handle everything for a few days. I promise to call if anything needs your personal attention and can't wait until you're back," Urban replied.

They had been coming to this restaurant for lunch for years whenever Urban could convince his wife to take a break from work long enough to grab a bite. After they both ordered, he reached across the table and took her hand in his.

"You won't regret it. A couple of days away did me good and it will do you good too. As soon as this all calms down, we'll take a break together."

"Well, I do plan to go to Senator Grant's fundraiser in D.C., and I assume you'll be going with me."

"Though I believe you deserve a getaway, don't you think it's a little too soon for us both to be out of town at the same time? I think we should skip this one and just send a check. I'm sure there will be other events during the campaign."

Urban figured this wasn't going to be an easy sell. His wife lived for functions like the senator's fundraiser gala. Since he was pro big business, everyone who was anyone in the business world would be there, not to mention other powerful politicians and the occasional celebrity.

"You know how much I enjoy these parties. I have no intention of missing it," Margaret stated.

"Well, if you must go, I could stay behind and keep an eye on things."

Margaret smiled. "Are you really that worried all of the sudden about leaving town with the crisis still unfolding, or are you trying to avoid going? I'm sorry you don't like formal events as much as I do, and I do appreciate you humoring me all these years. You look so handsome in a tux that I enjoy showing you off to my peers."

"I would prefer not to go. However, in this instance, I wouldn't want you to worry about being gone, so I'm happy to hold down the fort."

"What would people think if I showed up alone, without my adoring husband? The rumors would fly, especially if anyone caught wind of our two separate spouseless weekend getaways."

"Let's play it one day at a time for now. We can discuss this again when you get back." He would have to come up with a better strategy in order to win this argument.

"Very well. Where's the waiter? I'm very busy

today."

Urban flagged down the waiter and expressed their desire to speed things up. The waiter apologized and rushed off to check on their order.

For once, Urban wasn't offended when his wife pulled out her cell phone and began making calls. He hoped he'd done the right thing convincing her to leave town. Not only would that allow him to deal with the FBI if they returned or called, he truly hated seeing the fatigue in her beautiful eyes and the emergence of worry lines in her impeccable complexion.

"I hope you're happy. My assistant is working on the arrangements for my weekend at the spa as we speak."

"I am." Urban smiled as he reached for her hand again just as she pulled it away and stood to leave.

"If there's any hope of getting out of the office by the end of the week, I don't have time to sit around here all day and wait for lunch. Be a dear and have them box my salad, and you can bring it back to the office for me when you're done."

Urban nodded and watched his wife walk away.

TWENTY-SIX

Devyn didn't want to annoy her boss, but it had been over twenty-four hours since Conroy left a message with Senator Grant's staff asking him to call in regards to Aaron Truscott's university recommendation letter. She knocked on his door and waited until he told her to come in.

"Sorry to bother you, sir, but I was wondering if you've heard from Senator Grant yet?"

"I would have told you if I had, but now that you're here sit down. We'll give him another try."

When Conroy identified himself and provided the reason for his call, he was immediately transferred to the same senior staff member he had talked to the day before.

"I apologize for the delay, Agent Conroy, but we can't seem to locate any record of a request for a university admittance recommendation for an Aaron Truscott for the time frame you mentioned. We can't even find a copy of the letter that supposedly came out of this office. If it's not too much trouble could you scan, and e-mail us a copy of the letter in question? Maybe it would help us in tracking down the supporting documentation or perhaps jog someone's memory," the staffer stated.

Conroy said they would and jotted down the staffer's e-mail address. He asked that Senator Grant call him back either way, and then disconnected.

"Sorry, Nash. It seems like we're getting the political run-around. Send a copy of the letter to them and maybe that'll generate a response," Conroy stated, handing Devyn the sticky note with the information jotted down.

"I'll bet if you gave me ten minutes alone in a room with the good senator, I could jog his memory," Devyn fumed.

"I have no doubt, but as I've reminded you repeatedly, we better play this by the book until we have something solid linking the senator to Coterie. Even if we tie him to Aaron, who committed a laundry list of crimes in Arizona, there is no definitive link between Aaron and Coterie yet. Morgan felt certain that the backhand she got from Candace or Janice or whoever she is was due to regrets over her killing Aaron, but that doesn't prove anything. If Morgan misread the woman, the fact that Candace killed him would indicate they were not playing on the same team."

"All valid points, sir, but there are way too many threads weaving all of these players together for them not to be connected in some way."

"Agreed. All I'm saying is to tread lightly around the senator until we obtain solid evidence. I'd prefer to not be ordered to back off again when I'm convinced we're on the right track. I don't want him to slip through our fingers because we're over-zealous or sloppy."

Devyn promised to be discrete in regards to Senator Grant and left her boss's office feeling frustrated. There was a connection. She was certain, but she also suspected the senator might be an unwitting pawn and not a member of Coterie. She wasn't sure what he would have to gain. His family's fortune was massive. He liked the limelight. He didn't seem like the type to be in a secretive criminal organization when he didn't need money, and any notoriety that might result wouldn't be the type he would be looking for.

"Has Conroy heard anything back from Senator Grant on the letter?" Nick asked as she approached.

"Nope. He got the run-around from his staff. Anything from Tanner on Aaron's resume?"

"He's out on another op right now. I'm sure he'll check the evidence log as soon as he can and get a copy of Aaron's resume to us."

Devyn looked at her list. The banks were still not cooperating in tracing the deceased assassin, Frank Soto's, large bank deposits. Frank blew the Risky Research case wide open when he tried to kill a vitamin supplement researcher at her uncle's ranch in Wyoming. Unfortunately, he divulged little information about Coterie's members to Devyn. And the only information they had learned about Frank post-mortem was his last name, he hailed from Puerto Rico, and he had been paid well for his services.

So far, the APB on Janice Green and Candace Rogers had yielded nothing. Devyn and Nick had called nearly every pharmaceutical and medical research company in the U.S., including Puerto Rico and none reported any unusual happenings or reported any new hires meeting Janice or Candice's description.

Digging into Aaron's past turned up some interesting leads, but so far nothing tying him to Coterie. There were still a number of gaping holes in his life to fill in.

"You can look at that list until your eyes cross, but we'll still have nothing," Nick said, interrupting her thoughts.

"You're right. I need to step away for a bit and clear my mind. So, how did Morgan like the caveman routine you pulled yesterday?"

"I have no idea what you're talking about."

"Come on, Nick. No one is more adverse to PDAs than you, so for you to give Morgan a kiss like that in front of everyone, you were clearly marking your territory."

"PDAs?"

"You know, public displays of affection."

"Maybe I was wrong. Hand over that list. It could be worth another look."

TWENTY-SEVEN

For the first time in Sofia's adult life, she purposely waited to go into work until she was sure other people would be in the building. Arriving exceptionally early to avoid Trevor hadn't turned out too well, so she was willing to give the coward's way a shot.

She hoped Trevor was fearful enough of J.R. that he wouldn't try to kill her, especially without provocation. They had definitely gotten off on the wrong foot and the tension had yet to ease. The man made the hairs on the back of her neck stand at attention whenever she was in the same room with him.

When she stepped out of the elevator she immediately noticed that Trevor was not at his desk. She looked over at her door, wondering if he was in her office again. He should have had plenty of time to "sweep" her office for bugs if that was truly what he had been doing in there when she'd caught him in her office before hours.

Wandering down to the breakroom, she confirmed he wasn't there. When she returned, he still wasn't at his desk. Setting her briefcase on a chair, she took off her coat. If he was waiting for her she didn't want anything to hinder her self-defense.

Sofia turned the knob and then pushed the door hard. It flung open and bounced off of the door stop.

He wasn't hiding behind the door. She reached in, flipped the lights on, and scanned the interior of the room before crossing the threshold. Nothing.

Feeling ridiculous, she entered her office and checked her private en-suite. Finding it empty, she went back to Trevor's desk, gathered her belongings, and returned to her office. As she set her brief case on the desk, she noticed a sheet of paper on the chair seat.

Had to take care of something for J.R. I'll be back in the office on Monday—Trevor

Sofia was so relieved she wouldn't have to see him for the next few days that she didn't even care that her "assistant" didn't run it by her first before deciding to take on another project. Besides, she was fairly certain she didn't really want to know what he was taking care of for J.R.

Her meeting yesterday with Carson had taken a huge emotional toll on her. Not only was she forced to relive that horrible night, but whenever she did she struggled with the knowledge that she hadn't cried or experienced any sadness over her mother's death, only anger at the woman for taking away her limited freedom.

Sofia had come to terms with her mother's addictions and associated problems early on. She had learned to take care of herself and had mastered the art of avoiding the predators her mother brought into their home, but her death was unforgivable.

Thanks to Verda, Sofia had developed skills, self-respect, and a routine. She had no one to answer to and came and went as she pleased. Foster care changed everything. No one wanted to take on a troubled fifteen-year-old girl. She wasn't surprised to get short term families who saw to her physical needs, but who demonstrated no desire to love her. Most of the families were embarrassed to have anyone in their care hanging out at an after-school center for youth at risk, so she was forced to sneak off to spend time with Verda. Some temporary homes were too far away for her to make the journey at all, taking away the only stability she had ever found.

Pushing the thoughts out of her mind, she picked up her phone.

"Kelly, Trevor called in sick today. I need you to cover for him. Thanks."

The thought of having one of her eager perky interns at her reception desk and providing assistance for the next few days lifted Sofia's spirits. She believed her clients would appreciate the substitute as well.

Sofia retrieved the small slip of paper she kept in her wallet. A day without Trevor looking over her shoulder was the perfect opportunity to start working on her exit strategy.

TWENTY-EIGHT

Urban loved his wife and cherished her above all else, but he was relieved that she would be heading to the airport in a few hours. She deserved some relaxation and so did he. Her obsession with trying to find someone responsible for the near collapse of their company was making life more difficult for him. Juggling his wife's crisis and Coterie's desires were turning into two incompatible activities.

J.R. had called him yesterday to check if Margaret was still talking to the FBI, asking too many questions, and planning to attend Senator Grant's fundraiser. Urban happily reported there had been no further contact with the FBI, and that she would be departing the next day for her favorite Santa Fe spa for a few days of rest and relaxation. He hoped that would squelch any of J.R.'s concerns. Unfortunately, he had to admit to J.R. that he hadn't been able to dissuade her from attending the fundraiser, but he was still working on it.

Urban was certain that when Margaret returned she would be more focused on moving forward and saving her company than digging into the past. With Margaret out of pocket for a few days, if the FBI called he would convince them that GCF was simply one of Maggie Blair's suppliers and they were appalled to discover the company had been cutting corners and using a dangerous product.

"Mr. Blair," his assistant interrupted.

"Yes?"

"Mrs. Blair would like to go over a few things with you before she leaves for the weekend. When can I tell her you're available?"

He wasn't surprised by the summons. She was a micro-manager. She would want to go over every detail again before she left.

"Tell her I'll be right down."

When Urban entered his wife's office he was more convinced than ever that this weekend away alone was exactly what she needed. As he approached, she stopped pacing and let him pull her into his embrace.

"Margaret, quit worrying. It's only two nights away over the weekend. There is nothing that can happen that I can't handle. I know you well enough after all these years to be able to determine what you would do in most situations and what to run by you before acting. I promise I'll call if something important comes up."

"I'm sorry. I seldom take a weekend off and it feels especially wrong during this crisis."

"That's why you need it now. We've done all we can to slow the decline. I truly believe we've hit the bottom, and when you get back, we'll have even more work to do to rebuild. Rest, relax, and come back ready to fight."

"You're right, and you do know me well," she said as she stepped out of his embrace.

"So, is there anything specific to discuss, or were you going to try to bail out at the last minute?"

Urban could tell by the sheepish look on his wife's face that pulling the plug on the trip had crossed her mind. She ignored his question as she dug through a small stack of papers on her desk until she found several sheets of paper clipped together.

"Here, the top sheet is a copy of the flight manifest our pilot e-mailed, and the second sheet is my resort reservation. My cell phone will be nearby as much as possible, but if I don't answer and you need me, the resort manager's number is listed on the sheet."

Urban took the two sheets of paper and folded them until he could fit them in his inside jacket pocket.

"Can I take you to the airport?"

"I've already called for the driver, but if you'd like to ride along and your schedule is free, I would love to have you join me."

"I finished my last meeting for the day before you summoned me. I'll let Jean know I'm going to the airport, and I'll meet you in the lobby."

Urban had one more meeting, but he'd have Jean reschedule. He treasured any time spent with his workaholic wife. He also wanted to make sure she didn't change her mind before she got on the jet. She needed to get away until the dust settled, and he intended to ensure she did. He wasn't positive how paranoid and dangerous J.R. could be, and he had no intention of finding out.

TWENTY-NINE

Sofia's line rang four times. Deciding that Kelly must have stepped away from her desk, Sofia answered the phone. "Buyers Choice Foundation, how may I direct your call?"

"Sofia, darling, join me for lunch," J.R. cooed.

The call caught Sofia off guard. "That might be a little difficult unless you happen to be in D.C.," she replied.

"I am, and I'm parked outside your office. Come join me."

"It's a little late for lunch, but my schedule is open for the rest of the day. I'll be right down as soon as I can track down Kelly."

When they were apart, Sofia vowed to distance herself emotionally from J.R., but the second he called, her resolve always weakened. He was her kryptonite, and she wasn't sure how to avoid exposure when she was so inexplicably drawn to him.

By the time Sofia gathered her purse and jacket and stepped outside her office, Kelly had returned. Her assistant smiled at her, making Sofia once again thrilled to be rid of Trevor.

"Kelly, I can be reached on my cell if you need me. An unexpected meeting came up. I'll be back in a few hours."

"I'm sure everything will be fine here," Kelly replied. "It looks like it'll be a quiet afternoon."

The positive and friendly vibe from the young intern made Sofia pause before stepping into the elevator. If she could only convince J.R. to remove Trevor from her business, she would try to recruit the competent young woman to join the company full-time once she finished her Master's program.

Sofia was growing weary of all the violence, fear, and drama in her life. She could benefit from a more positive atmosphere in the office, for her own sanity as well as for the image she preferred to exude to her clients.

As Sofia approached the dark luxury sedan with heavily tinted windows, the back door opened, but no one got out. She slid into the seat and closed the door. Before she could buckle her belt, J.R. pulled her into a strong embrace and captured her lips in a long, yet demanding kiss.

"I've missed you very much," he said as he released her. "Please tell me you've missed me, too?"

"We saw each other less than a week ago, but as much as I don't want to admit it, yes, I've missed you, too."

"Why do you fight the inevitable, Sofia? We're perfect for each other. We're destined to be together."

"I've worked hard to be financially and emotionally independent. Exerting complete control over my own life is paramount to me. I don't want to need anyone, and I can't allow anyone to make decisions for me."

He smiled and took her hand. His touch sent electricity surging through her body. No one had ever touched her in kindness. The tenderness in his expression made her want to give in, but why to this man? He could be so caring and kind to her, but she had witnessed the ruthless side of him and those images made her shudder.

"Are you cold?"

"A little," she lied.

"Turn the air conditioning down," J.R. demanded of the driver as he wrapped his arm around her and pulled her close.

The drive to the restaurant was short. Soon Sofia found herself sitting across from J.R. in a dimly lit corner of the exclusive bistro. She had never been to this restaurant before and wondered how he was even aware of its existence since he preferred to spend as little time as possible in D.C.

As J.R. order their beverages, Sofia debated if she should ask about Trevor's assignment. She didn't actually care and suspected it might be best to be oblivious. What she really wanted was the surly and intimidating man out of her life.

"Is there any chance that Trevor's new project is permanent, and I can hire my own replacement for Justine?"

J.R. laughed. His tone was rich and warm, making her heart flutter. "Sofia, I explained my concerns for your safety. Let me take care of you. I cannot bear the thought of losing you."

"I appreciate your concern, but I can take care of myself. If you care for me as you say you do, remove Trevor from my office."

Her eyes locked on his for a long moment. She wished she could ascertain what was going through his mind. If his motives were sincere, she was touched that someone wanted to protect her for once, but she couldn't shake the suspicion that Trevor was inserted into her life to spy on her.

"If it's that important to you, he won't return. Please be vigilant, Sofia. Our enemies are growing and the authorities are getting too close. If anything happened to you, I don't know what I would do. You are the first woman to truly capture my heart."

"Thank you. It's difficult to run my business when it's clear he makes my clients as uncomfortable as he does me. Justine charmed potential customers and donors. Charisma and the ability to encourage donors to write big checks is part of the job, and Trevor is severely lacking in those departments. His people skills are nonexistent."

"Since I agreed to remove Trevor, I hope you'll consider my proposal, which is why I made the trip to D.C. today."

The conversation stopped as the waiter delivered the wine and poured two glasses once gaining J.R.'s approval. The waiter took their order and scurried off.

"I won't leave all I've built to be your mistress."

"I understand, and that's one of the things I love most about you. Some woman would consider such a scenario to be a career choice, whereas you consider it an insult. Whatever you give of yourself to me is genuine and that touches me deeply."

Sofia sipped her wine, watching him over the rim of her glass. She didn't respond, waiting for him to continue.

"As you know, I've been working on building a new pharmaceutical plant in Brazil. It's nearly complete, and I'm in the process of selecting key management and other employees to get the facility up and running. I want you to manage the facility in Brazil. I'll be there often to assist you in anything need, but there is no one I trust more than you. You would be completely in charge."

She was stunned. J.R. had told her about his newest project, but she had no idea he would want her involved.

"I'm not sure if I'm ready to give up my foundation."

"You wouldn't have to relinquish all control. Find someone you trust to run it in your absence. Check in as necessary until you decide if you want to stay in Brazil permanently or once the factory is up and running, return to your business."

"How soon do you need a decision?"

"I would like you on the ground within two weeks. Some key staff is already there."

"I'll think about it, but it will be difficult to find someone to head up Buyers Choice on such short notice. I could have trusted Justine, but she's dead."

Sofia stated the last word with more venom than she had intended. She had no proof J.R. had anything to do with her assistant's death, but she couldn't force the suspicion out of her mind.

J.R. pulled his hand back, and the smile disappeared. "You must move on. Think about my proposal. I need a decision soon. The authorities are closing in on us. Remember, Brazil has no extradition."

"What about Coterie? Am I no longer essential?"

"Your service has been invaluable in multiple ways, but I fear Coterie's usefulness may have run its course. Max's plane and special skills have come in handy in the past. Preston had become a parasite, and I'm struggling to find any benefit from Urban or Terrance."

Sofia wasn't sure how to respond. If J.R. no longer saw any use for Urban and Terrance, would they be allowed to walk away? Something told her that wouldn't be an option. If she refused to go to Brazil, would she no longer be needed either? She wanted to believe J.R.'s love for her was real, but would it be enough to protect her?

THIRTY

Margaret arrived late to the Santa Fe spa. The entire facility exuded a sense of serenity. Her suite offered the perfect combination of soothing aromas, natural sounds that encouraged rest and relaxation, lavish décor, and plenty of expensive wine chilling and waiting to be served. After several glasses, she drifted off to sleep with the sounds of a gentle spring bubbling in the background.

Slowly opening her eyes, Margaret rolled over and looked at the clock. She was surprised by the time displayed. She seldom slept this late into the morning, and the luxury felt simply indulgent.

The options for her day's itinerary where elegantly printed on a menu card and had been slipped under her door sometime during the middle of the night. The flow of activities would proceed at a leisurely pace but would keep her day filled, preventing her from thinking about work.

Shortly after calling for room service a waiter arrived with a cart and laid out her breakfast on a small table on her private deck overlooking the stark, yet stunning landscape. Once halfway through her first cup of coffee she picked up her cell phone and punched in the first number in her contact list.

"Good morning, Urban. You were right, I did need this, and all I've done so far is get a sound night of sleep. Now I'm sitting on my private deck enjoying a delightful cup of coffee and scrumptious hot fresh pastries."

"I'm so happy you were able to get some rest. I wish I were there with you, but I knew you wouldn't relax without me holding down the fort. And speaking of the fort, everything is quiet and running smoothly here. Not surprisingly since it's Saturday morning. My phone hasn't rung even once. I'm getting caught up on my review of last quarter's report. So, please put the company out of your mind for the next forty-eight hours and relax."

"I will. I suspect you helped my assistant organize my day. All the services I enjoy are scheduled. I have a facial, body wrap, massage, and a Tibetan sound therapy session. Tonight, I plan a long soak in an absolutely decadent spa pool here in my private serenity room. If I can fit it in tomorrow I plan to go into town to do a little shopping. The galleries here are magnificent."

"I'm glad we chose your activities well. I wanted to make sure this weekend was as beneficial and enjoyable for you as possible. You deserve it."

"Thank you. And, Urban, I know I haven't told you or showed you lately, but I do love you."

"I love you, too. Now relax, enjoy, and come back refreshed. I'll see you soon."

Margaret set her phone down and continued to sip her coffee. She probably did take her husband for granted, but running a company like Maggie Blair, Inc. was stressful, especially since the Giant Cactus Foods catastrophe.

She needed to be completely focused at all times. One lapse and everything she spent years building had been severely damaged.

Margaret seldom stooped so low or played the usual dirty corporate games, but there were a few people who owed her favors and she would call in as many as it took to shut GCF down forever. There was no way she would allow GCF to come out unscathed even if the guilty party was dead. Someone must pay for her losses.

THIRTY-ONE

"Hey there, cowboy. Thought I'd call early in case you have a hot date tonight," Devyn stated when Gage answered the phone.

"Not likely since I'm here and you're there," he replied. "How's your weekend going so far?"

"I'm bored to death. I'm getting better physically each day, but the ribs and feet would still scream if I went back to running or headed to the mountains for a hike. Being so idle, drives me absolutely crazy."

His deep rich laugh made her yearn to be with him, to feel his strong arms around her, to enjoy one of his long sensual kisses that made her toes curl.

"I'll bet. Maybe you should take a few vacation days and come to Wyoming for a little break. I'm sure I can keep you entertained. I bet I can even teach a city girl like you how to ride. I have a handsome gelding with a great disposition that'll treat you right."

Devyn smiled at the thought of being "entertained" by Gage and learning to ride did sound exciting, but she wouldn't take him up on his offer.

"As tempting as that sounds, there are so many loose ends blowing around in the wind on the Risky Research investigation that I'm afraid the whole thing is going to come unraveled at any moment. Nick's good, but he's a little distracted at the moment with Morgan back in his life and planning their wedding, so I need to stick to the case and stay focused. Besides, there are too many leads for one person to follow alone. Unfortunately, judges, lawyers, bankers, and senatorial office staff all think they should get the weekend off, which shuts me down."

"Hang in there. If you can't come to me, I'll go to you as soon as my deputy gets back from his honeymoon. I've got a great gig here, but there's more to life than the job—even your job, Devyn."

Devyn didn't answer immediately. She was riddled with guilt. Clearly, Gage was willing to meet her at least half way, but so far, she hadn't made much of an effort. She did want to explore where their relationship could go, but giving up her independence wouldn't be easy. She had never had to consider anyone else's schedule, wants, or needs and it was a bit of an adjustment.

"Be patient with me. I'm new to this relationship thing. I seldom take the easy route. When I finally find a man worth holding on to, of course, I had to choose one who lived in another state. A local guy would be far too simple."

"You know what they say, 'nothing worth having is ever easy,' but I'm willing to work at this, and I hope you are, too. I think we could truly have something special here."

"I do too. I can barely get you out of my mind enough to do my job, and I fear you may be even more entrenched in my heart."

"Wow—that was pretty good for a woman new to the 'relationship thing.'"

"Well, I meant it. You're seriously screwing up my focus."

"Thanks, that's the nicest thing you've ever said to me." Gage chuckled.

"Glad you took it that way because that's how I intended it, but often things come out the wrong way when I try to express my feelings. Heck, until you came back into my life, I didn't even realize I had any."

Devyn was always amazed at how easy it was to talk to Gage. Other than Morgan, she had never opened up to anyone as much. She never intended to bare her soul to this man. So far in her life, she hadn't allowed anyone close enough to break her heart, but it was too late. Gage possessed the power to destroy her.

"What'cha thinking?"

She tried to come up with something less embarrassing than the truth, but nothing came to mind. "I was wondering why you're so easy to talk to, and if you'll end up breaking my heart."

"That'll be up to you. But, at the moment the only thing I have a desire to break is this Gardner guy's nose. Has he been giving you anymore grief?"

Devyn was pleased to report she had successfully avoided any recent run-ins with the antagonistic agent, and she was even happier that Gage had changed the subject.

THIRTY-TWO

The day had been pure bliss and it wasn't quite over yet. Maggie reclined in the steaming personal hot tub in her private serenity room. With her hair confined in a towel wrapped like a turban, cool cucumber slices placed over her eyes, and Tibetan singing bowl music gently drifting through the room, it was difficult not to fall asleep.

Despite the spa staff's best efforts to keep her distracted, thoughts of work seeped into her mind, but at least as she plotted and planned her strategy for the upcoming weeks, the prognosis was positive. If nothing else, the weekend's activities rejuvenated her fighting spirit and forced from her mind some of the negativity and fear of losing the company.

While slowly rebuilding client trust in their meals, she planned to expand the number of gyms across the country and maybe open them up under a different name. The Maggie Blair, Inc. gyms were a big money maker, not as high-grossing as the meal plan and counseling part of the business, but still substantial and capable of propping up the other sectors until the crisis passed.

Once memories of the deadly sweetener faded from the public's memory she could incorporate the new gyms under the Maggie Blair umbrella. The company wouldn't enjoy the same profits it had the past two years, but by expanding the gyms she was certain that within three years, the entire company would be back on solid ground.

As the sounds of the singing bowls relaxed her mind and coaxed her into a meditative state, business faded further from her thoughts. A calm sense of peace settled over her, forcing all the tension from her muscles and negative energy from her body. Sleep threatened to engulf her as she slid lower into the soothing water.

Margaret wasn't sure how long she'd been in the water but figured it hadn't been that long or her attendant would have come for her. She wasn't anxious to leave the warm embrace of the swirling waters, but she was starting to feel a little hungry and the quality of the food at the spa made mealtimes a special activity.

She leisurely pondered the evening's menu as if in a dream. For the first time in years she missed the simpler times when she and Urban possessed far less wealth and far fewer worries. They shared such big dreams in those early years of marriage, and their excitement for their future had made every day a new adventure.

Yes, that's how she needed to look at the current crisis, as a new adventure they could tackle together. Maybe in the processes of saving the company they could rekindle the passion in their marriage.

~*~

The man flipped the sign outside the door to read "Privacy Please," before slipping silently into the dimly lit room. The sound of the harmonic overtones from the Tibetan singing bowls reverberated throughout the serene space. Aromas from exotic oils and incense assaulted his senses, momentarily distracting him from his mission.

As he shut the door, it clicked loudly.

"It's about time. I thought maybe you had forgotten about me," the woman in the hot tub stated.

"Of course not, Ms. Blair, just continue to relax while I prepare your robe," he replied.

Cucumber slices obscured her vision. He silently walked up behind her and knelt down. Placing his hands on her shoulders he began to gently knead her muscles.

"Oh, that's wonderful," she said as she slid lower into the water.

He continued to masterfully massage her shoulders until her body became limp from complete relaxation. He slowly eased her lower and lower into the steaming cauldron. The water began to lap at her chin. He could feel her start to tense.

"That's enough. I'm ready to get out now," she demanded as she tried unsuccessfully to push herself up from the tub.

She was so reclined that her feet were unable to get any purchase on the sloped surface to counteract the downward pressure he exerted on her shoulders. She struggled against him, but her position and his size made the attempt futile.

He continued to push, utilizing mostly his palms to avoid leaving fingertip bruises on her unblemished skin until her face was under water. Screaming would only allow water into her lungs and would be heard by no one. She continued to thrash, but as planned, any noise she made would be disguised by the jets churning water through the tub and the unique music floating through the humid air.

As the last remnants of life drained from her body he eased up on the pressure. She didn't respond. The job was done.

THIRTY-THREE

Devyn hated admitting her cowardice, but she was relieved when she and Nick arrived in the parking lot at the same time. Walking through the vast open office area with him would deter any confrontations with Gardner.

"I certainly hope your weekend was more exciting than mine," Devyn said as she and Nick exited the elevator.

"We stayed home all weekend. You should have called Morgan. I'm sure she would have taken you shopping for whatever it is you think will make Gage lose his mind over you."

Devyn rolled her eyes. "I'm not sure that would help. First, we need to be in the same state together and, so far, that has proven to be a challenge."

"Try harder and quit obsessing about this case. Leave town and enjoy a little romance. I understand there isn't cell reception everywhere in Wyoming, but Gage is the sheriff. I'm confident he's always reachable by radio if not by phone. I promise I'll contact you if something breaks in the case."

"Maybe I'll try to surprise him this upcoming weekend if we don't get a break before then."

"The job isn't everything. You deserve a personal life as much as the next person. What if he's the one and you let him get away because of this ghost we've been chasing and may never catch?"

"Hasn't your tone changed? I bet you wouldn't have said that last month, pre-Morgan."

"Maybe not. Fortunately, I received a little reminder in Arizona about what's truly important, and it isn't this." Nick waved his hand in an arc encompassing the bustling room.

At times, like now, Devyn wished she had the old Nick back. She used to want him to open up a little about personal stuff, but now that he and Morgan were back together, he offered more relationship advice than she cared to hear.

"You know, I kind of miss Gordo," Devyn stated as they approached their desks in an attempt to steer the conversation away from her love life or lack thereof. "I didn't eat breakfast this morning, and I'm starving."

"Morgan's dropping off some papers for me to sign in a bit. Do you want her to pick up something for you? I'm sure she wouldn't mind."

"I'll text her." Devyn checked her messages and wasn't surprised to find nothing of importance. Any news from the senator's office would come directly through Conroy, and the Cayman bank they had contacted concerning where the deposits into Frank Soto's account came from, would offer up nothing without a lot more pressure.

"I can't decide which dead end to grab a hold of this morning," Devyn pondered.

"Maybe Conroy found something. He's heading our way," Nick replied.

Devyn swiveled around in her chair. Conroy approached, his expression unreadable as usual. Hopefully, she wasn't in any trouble. She couldn't think of any toes she might have stepped on over the past few days.

"Nash, Melonis," he said nodding at each in turn.

"Sir, happy Monday," Devyn replied.

A crooked grin eased across his lips briefly before he jumped in.

"Margaret Blair of Maggie Blair, Inc., was found dead in a hot tub at a luxury spa in Santa Fe. It appears she fell asleep and drowned, but the authorities are investigating and, of course, an autopsy will be performed. There are no obvious external wounds or bruising."

"Was Urban with her?" Devyn asked.

"No. He claims he stayed behind to watch the company so his wife would be able to relax. The local police reported he was extremely distraught by the news, and a number of employees can corroborate his alibi."

"You don't believe her death was accidental, do you?" Devyn asked.

"Well, the timing sure makes me seriously question the likelihood. I relayed everything we suspect to the authorities in Santa Fe and asked to be kept in the loop.""

Had someone decided to silence Margaret Blair for talking to the FBI? Who, besides her husband, was even aware of the meeting? After their brief interview, Devyn concluded that Margaret likely knew nothing about GCF or its connections to Coterie, but she hadn't been as certain about Urban.

Devyn wasn't an expert on relationships, by any means, but she had gotten the impression that Urban was thoroughly in love with his wife. She was having a difficult time picturing Urban killing her, with or without the alibi. The husband is always the first to be scrutinized, so it would've been a risky move on his part, especially on the heels of her and Nick's visit to the couple.

"Where do we go from here?" Nick asked.

"After what we learned or didn't learn about Aaron's connection to Senator Grant and with one of his biggest donors showing up dead, I'd sure love to get someone inside that fundraiser," Conroy stated.

"He has to be connected to all of this somehow," Devyn added.

"I can get Nick placed with the company providing security for the fundraiser, but I'm not sure how much good that would do."

"I can get in," Morgan stated as she walked up and dropped a packet of papers on Nick's desk and a breakfast burrito on Devyn's.

"No." Nick shook his head.

"Wait a minute. Let's hear what she has to say," Conroy stated.

"My father contributed heavily and was a big supporter of Carson Grant's father, George. I haven't continued that tradition, but I'll bet with the right donation I'd get a quick invite to next weekend's exclusive fundraiser. If they look into my family history, which I assume they would when honing the invitee list, they will make the connection immediately between my father and me."

"I don't want you anywhere near him. At worst he's part of Coterie. At best he's being manipulated by them. Either way he could be dangerous," Nick stated.

"I can't imagine I would be in any danger at the fundraiser. There will be plenty of security there."

"She's right. You'd be there to keep an eye on her," Devyn added.

Nick gave Devyn a scowl that clearly indicated she wasn't helping and should stay out of it.

"Normally I don't like involving civilians, but I agree with Morgan. She won't be in any danger with Capitol police, local police, hotel security, and the senator's private security crawling all over the facility. We'd put a discrete wire on her and who knows what she could learn milling around," Conroy said.

Devyn remained quiet. She doubted having Morgan attend a fundraiser for a few hours could possibly put her in any danger, but this was something Morgan and Nick needed to work out on their own. Nick would definitely not appreciate her input.

"Nick, I want to do this. If I can help in any way to identify Coterie, I think it's worth a shot. Remember, before I met you, I worked in the pharmaceutical industry. The next time this group strikes it could be someone I know. My attendance won't likely yield anything, but maybe someone will let something slip. I still have a lot of friends in the area, so I'm sure I can get one of them to go with me if I can score an invite."

Devyn, Morgan, and Conroy turned their attention to Nick.

"I suppose in the end I don't actually have a say in this, do I?"

"No," Morgan replied sweetly as she reached over and gently caressed his cheek.

"Well, with that settled, let's go see if we can request enough seized drug money to make a big enough campaign contribution to get you an invite," Conroy said to Morgan, motioning for her to follow.

Nick slumped in his chair.

"I don't like the way the other agents ogle her as she walks through the room, but this makes me really not want her coming down here at all. She has this notion that this time we should be more involved in each other's lives, including work. Helping in the Risky Research case is way too involved for my comfort level."

"Don't worry, she'll be fine," Devyn assured.

"Is that what you thought when you let her drive you to the hospital in Phoenix?"

The statement stung, but it was true. She would beat herself up for that decision for the rest of her life. Thankfully, Morgan had survived and this time would be no different.

THIRTY-FOUR

Sofia had wanted some time alone over the weekend to think about J.R.'s proposal, but instead he had whisked her off to Puerto Rico in his private jet. He claimed touring his Puerto Rico facilities would help her decide if she wanted to manage his similar property in Brazil, but aside from a quick visit to his plant, the rest of the activities were clearly selected to win her over. She should have enjoyed the outings in his yacht, dining in San Juan's most exclusive hot spots, and riding horses on the beach with J.R., but her pending decision weighed heavily on her mind.

During the tour of his pharmaceutical plant he explained his vision for the facility in Brazil, which would be nearly identical. She had never been to Brazil, but working closely with J.R. to start up a new factory would give her time to determine if a life with him was worth giving up everything she had striven for her entire adult life.

The most immediate obstacle preventing her from committing to his proposal was the idea of handing over management of her company to someone else while she was away. She employed a great staff, but she had always kept a tight rein on day-to-day operations and wasn't sure anyone currently on the payroll could step in without a lot of training. It didn't sound like time to train someone was accounted for in J.R.'s plan.

When she strode out of the elevator at Buyer's Choice, she was a little surprised, and definitely pleased, to find Kelly sitting at Justine's desk. J.R. promised Trevor wouldn't be back. She had remained cautiously optimistic all weekend, but not convinced.

"I wasn't sure if you still wanted me to cover for Trevor, but since I didn't see him this morning I thought I'd sit here until one of you told me otherwise," Kelly said.

"Trevor has taken another opportunity at my urging. Once you're finished with your thesis for your graduate work would you be interested in full-time employment here?" Sofia asked.

"I would love the opportunity. I realize Justine's shoes will be hard to fill, but I promise to give you my all," Kelly replied enthusiastically.

"I need someone with your education, skills, professionalism, and to be honest, your look. Trevor was making the clients nervous. He should be working for the Secret Service, not at the reception desk of a lobbying firm. He was recommended to me by an associate, and I was desperate, but I'm glad he's gone."

Kelly chuckled. "I'm glad to hear you say that. He gave me and everyone else on staff the heebie-jeebies."

"He certainly lacked your interpersonal communications skills. He was only intended to be a temporary bridge until I found someone I was comfortable with. Anyway, let's talk later about how many hours you can spare until your studies are done."

Kelly thanked her again as she made her way into her office. Despite her original euphoria with Trevor's absence, a sick feeling resided deep down in her gut. She hoped Kelly wouldn't end up sharing the same fate as Justine. She also feared that J.R. hadn't caved as easily as she thought. Was Trevor still "protecting" her? It was even more dangerous having him lurking out of sight than sitting outside her door. She hoped she hadn't made a huge mistake in demanding his removal.

Pushing the thoughts of Trevor out of her mind, she sat down at her desk and picked up the newspaper Kelly had placed in her inbox. She could read it online but preferred to keep up with what was happening in the city the old-fashioned way.

The front-page story caught her eye immediately. She gasped as she stared at the headline.

President of Giant Weight Loss Company, Maggie Blair, Inc., Found Dead in Santa Fe Spa.

She quickly read through the story. The death was still under investigation. The authorities were unwilling to speculate, but the reporter had no problem doing just that. The writer insinuated the death could be suicide on the heels of the crisis brought on by the Giant Cactus Foods scandal.

Sofia believed differently.

Rereading the story, she struggled to understand why. Urban's wife had talked to the FBI and was digging for the truth behind Giant Cactus, but surely that wasn't serious enough to have her silenced.

Sofia didn't know what to do or think. She couldn't call Urban and offer her condolences nor could she accuse J.R. of being involved. She had made it clear to him that she suspected he was behind Justine's death. He never admitted to any involvement, but he didn't deny her accusations either. She hoped Margaret Blair's death was accidental or suicide, but the timing of Trevor's departure was too much of a coincidence to ignore.

She walked over to her window. Scanning the area below, she saw nothing. Yes, she may have made a critical error in demanding Trevor's dismissal. A line from *Godfather II* ran through her mind as she searched outside for any sign of Trevor watching her: *keep your friends close and your enemies closer*.

THIRTY-FIVE

Devyn couldn't believe Conroy actually agreed to allow her to travel to Washington D.C. She was ordered to stay away from the senator, the fundraiser, and Nick while he was on duty, but at least she would be on the periphery, listening and watching.

She, Gordo, and Fitz would be in a van down the street providing surveillance and any support Nick requested. They would monitor everything coming through Morgan's wire and tiny camera, searching for suspicious activity. Most importantly, Devyn was determined to ensure Morgan's safety.

Conroy received official approval from his superior at the FBI in D.C. for the side operation and his assurance that no one on the ground would know about Morgan's wire. Conroy feared any extreme loyalty to the senator could put her in danger or at least ruin any attempt to get information, making the whole mission pointless.

Before heading to D.C. later in the week, Devyn planned to make a detour to Denver to pay Urban Blair a personal visit. Conroy strongly advised her to be sensitive in case he was in no way connected to Coterie and simply a grieving widower with a crumbling empire. She'd play it his way, but her gut told her that Urban was up to his eyeballs in Coterie.

"Can you take me to the airport?" Nick asked.

"Sure, but I assumed Morgan would drive you,"

Devyn replied.

"Not a good idea. I don't like this whole plan one bit, and I don't want to argue with her anymore about it. She's determined to go through with it. I was hoping the large donation she made to the senator's campaign was too late to get her an invite, but as she predicted, an invitation showed up the next day by special courier."

"I'm not crazy about her being involved either, especially after what happened in Arizona. But let's face it. You and I possess a fraction of the political and social savvy as she does. She'll ease in seamlessly. She can read these people, and she might catch some subtle nuance I might miss even if I was in there. And we both know Morgan is much more likely to charm the senator or one of his cronies into talking than any female agent in this building, present company included."

"That's not helping, Devyn. She's tougher than she looks, smart, and resourceful. There'll be tons of security there, but I've got a bad feeling."

"I can't tell you not to worry, because I'm worried, too. Gordo, Fitz, and I have your back. I'll do everything I can from the periphery to keep her safe."

"I know you will, and I'm sure I'm overreacting, but it seems like Phoenix was just yesterday not a month ago. I'm still having nightmares about how close I came to losing her."

Devyn wasn't sure what else she could do or say to reassure Nick. She had agreed with Conroy that Morgan wouldn't be in any danger, but she couldn't dismiss Nick's gut any more than she could dismiss her own. She'd have to be on her toes.

"Learn all you can about the players. Keep me

informed, and I'll be there in a couple days after I pay my respects to Mr. Blair. I don't doubt his grief is genuine. My main objective is to determine if he buys the accident or suicide theories floating around. If not, I'd love to find out if he's willing to divulge who might be responsible."

"We'd better go so I don't miss my flight. Just get to D.C. as quick as you can. I'll be more comfortable with this whole thing once you get there. All the law enforcement agencies should be working together, but when politics are involved I can't help but question everyone's agenda and loyalty. I'm confident where yours lie."

Nick's words eased the doubts she had since returning from Arizona and relief swept through her. She worried Nick had lost some of his trust in her after what happened in Phoenix, so hearing that he would feel better once she arrived made her want to hug him, but she refrained.

"Morgan isn't flying out for another couple days, so try to relax until then. There will be nothing to worry about here except that I might pry some more of your deepest darkest secrets out of her over a tub of raw cookie dough.."

The furrows in Nick's forehead eased, and a nervous smile formed on his lips. "I can't believe I'm saying this, but if that's the least of my worries, I'll take it."

THIRTY-SIX

After giving Kelly several projects to work on in her absence, Sofia left her office and rode the elevator to the ground floor. She exited the building, searching every direction for any sign of Trevor or any other possible threat. Detecting nothing out of the ordinary, she caught the Metro to the National Mall.

Sofia took her time strolling around the monuments for the next hour until she was convinced she hadn't been followed. She returned to the Metro and rode the subway to a destination in southeast Washington, D.C. She had been to this specific neighborhood only once before and she hoped this would be the last.

She had visited a small shop a week ago to take care of a long overdue project. She wanted to be sure she had an exit strategy if her dealings with Coterie deteriorated or if she was exposed. If she needed to disappear she would do so as Miranda Baxter, a non-descript woman with mousy brown hair, blue eyes, thick glasses, and adult braces. Her new passport would show she was born in Iowa.

After exiting the Metro, she walked three blocks to a dilapidated store front claiming to sell second hand clothing. Entering the run-down shop, Sofia saw no other customers or employees. She rang the bell on the counter and after several minutes the same elderly man she dealt with the week before emerged from the back and motioned for her to follow him through a door into a separate non-public room.

The man retrieved a briefcase from a safe and set it on the counter. He popped the lid and waited silently while Sofia examined the contents which included a driver's license, passport, and the basic components of her new identity.

Sofia was amazed by the artistry. Her face on the documents was altered enough to not be detected with facial recognition software and matched the professionally constructed mask perfectly. The mask, a wig, colored contacts, a retainer that mimicked the look of braces, and eyeglasses completed the transformation.

"You're certain the chips embedded in the passport will work at any airport?" she stated, trying to hide her awe over his work.

"None of my products have ever failed," he replied.

Sofia pulled a thick envelope filled with one-hundred-dollar bills from her purse. She watched as he counted each one and examined random bills for authenticity.

"Nice doing business with you," he said as he held the door to the front of the shop open, indicating it was time for her to leave.

Cleary the transaction was complete and no further questions would be entertained by the man. She looked at the disguise and documents one more time before closing the lid on the briefcase and following him back into the used clothing portion of the shop.

The quality of the passport, driver's license, and disguise seemed flawless. Unfortunately, she was relying on the word of a criminal that the documents could get her out of the country and the disguise would hold up even if a photo of her in the mask was run through facial recognition software. The only way to be certain was to test them, and she had no intention of introducing Miranda Baxter to the world until absolutely necessary.

She prayed the day would never come when she needed the contents of the case, because if that day came, it would mean something had gone drastically wrong. With a mixture of relief and dread, Sofia exited the shop clutching the briefcase. She quickly made her way to the closest Metro stop and boarded the train. Retracing her route, she worked her way toward her office.

As she crossed the street at the end of the block she spotted a blonde man in a jogging suite with dark glasses. His body was partially obscured by an ice cream cart. He went through the motions of stretching. Despite the change in hair color and the baggy exercise wear, she instantly recognized Trevor. The bulk of his upper arms, the girth of his neck, and the arrogant jut of his chin could not conceal his true identity.

Debating whether or not she should confront him, Sofia walked slowly toward her building. She would love to call him out, but then again, it might be good to let him believe he had fooled her. She decided to ignore him, hoping he would foolishly re-use his current sad excuse for a disguise.

As Sofia rode the elevator up to her office, a bit of her old confidence returned. She was slowly getting a little control back over her life. Having an exit strategy only she was aware of, ridding Trevor from her business, and learning he still watched her gave her an upper hand. She would have preferred he was not around, but at least knowing his whereabouts would make it easier to protect herself if his intentions weren't as honorable as J.R. claimed.

THIRTY-SEVEN

The quick flight to Denver gave Devyn all the time she needed to plan how she would approach Urban. She called ahead and verified he hadn't come into the office at all since he received the news about Margaret's death.

With his home address programmed into her phone, Devyn drove her rental car to the exclusive gated neighborhood where he and his wife had resided for the past six years. The houses were impressive and the guard at the gate was thorough in his examination of her credentials.

Parking in the large circular off-street driveway, Devyn made her way to the massive double doors. Looking at the grand house in the beautiful neighborhood made her sympathy for Urban increase. He appeared to have it all, but a seemingly unrelated incident in another state robbed him of everything.

Devyn rang the doorbell. After several minutes, a small woman answered the door.

"May I help you?"

Devyn showed her badge. "I need to speak to Mr. Blair."

"This is not a good time. You must make an appointment for another day. Please call his office."

"It's imperative that I speak to him now."

"Who's there, Rosa," Urban yelled.

"A woman with the FBI."

"Might as well show her in." He lowered his voice.

Devyn followed the woman—whom she assumed was an employee based on the woman's attire—to a darkened den in the back of the house. Urban slouched in an uncomfortable-looking wingback chair with an empty glass and a half empty bottle of scotch resting on a coffee table next to his chair.

He motioned for her to take a seat. "Wanna drink?" he slurred as he poured two fingers of caramel colored liquid into his glass.

"No, thank you," Devyn replied, watching the grieving man clumsily attempt to recap the bottle.

She hoped he was sober enough to participate in a conversation and drunk enough for it to be an honest exchange. Even though she rehearsed what she was going to say, seeing Urban this way made her reassess her approach to the sensitive subject on her agenda. The last time she saw him he was impeccably dressed and groomed, confident, and comfortable in his empire. Now he looked sick, disheveled, and pathetic.

"I'm so sorry for your loss. I can't imagine how difficult this is for you. It was clear the first time I met the both of you how much you loved her."

"To Maggie," he said as he toasted no one.

Devyn's hopes of getting any useful information faded as the small motion of toasting nearly made him lose his balance despite being seated. Devyn held her breath as the dainty chair teetered back and forth. She assumed it must be Margaret's chair since it looked to small and too feminine for this man.

"Why are you here?" he demanded. "I talked to the investigators. Don't you share information?"

"Yes, but I wanted to speak to you directly. I'm sure they were asking for facts and an alibi. With the passing of a spouse in unwitnessed circumstances, I imagine they wanted to verify where you were at the time of the incident."

"Like I'd follow my Maggie to Sana Fe and drown her," he spit out with venom. "She's my world."

"I sensed that during our short visit, so I want your theory. No one knew your wife better than you."

He gazed up at Devyn through bloodshot eyes. The look in his expression was a complex mixture of grief, anger, and hatred. He blinked several times and downed the rest of his scotch in on long gulp. He reached for the bottle and poured the liquid nearly to the brim this time. She feared the conversation was over before it began.

"You wanna hear my theory?"

Devyn nodded and waited for him to continue.

"*Iss* my fault. My idea. I wish I hadna send her there. She worked so hard trying to save that stupid company. I jus wanted her to relax, take a load off."

His speech was getting worse by the minute as he struggled to focus and keep upright in his chair.

"What do you think happened?" Devyn asked.

"She was always careful, and she'd never kill herself. Too tough, too stubborn. Loved that company more than me." He hiccupped, and his shoulders sagged to the left.

"I'm sure she loved you more." Her heart went out to the man. Despite her belief he harbored some ties to Coterie, he was clearly suffering.

"Whada you know?" he spat.

"Not much," Devyn replied. "That's why I'm here. Do you think it was an accident?"

His eyes narrowed and bored into her. "*Iss* your fault," he whispered. "Git outta here. You got no right coming around after what you did," his voice rose from a near whisper to a roar.

He pushed himself up from his chair, and it tumbled over. He took several steps toward Devyn before crumbling into a heap on the carpet. He curled up into a ball and sobbed.

Devyn had never seen anyone so drunk, and she'd witnessed a lot of drunken behavior in her career. Clearly the flight to Denver had been a waste of time and money. She walked out into the hallway.

"Rosa, could you please come here?" Devyn asked.

The woman bustled into the room and rushed to Urban's side.

"Oh, Mr. Blair, you must go to your room and sleep."

He batted her arm away.

"Have you seen him this drunk before?" Devyn asked.

"Several times since Ms. Blair passed," she responded.

"Do you think we should call an ambulance?"

"No, he will be fine once he sleeps it off. I will go get a pillow and a blanket," Rosa replied as she rushed out of the room.

Devyn knelt down beside him. His sobbing ebbed, and he now mumbling incoherently. Devyn cocked her ear toward him, trying to understand his words. Though straining to listen, the closest she could make out was something about "jars sofa mess pay." It sounded like he repeated the odd phrase several times before he retched.

She stood and jumped back, pinching her noise to block the sour smell as much as possible, fearing the disgusting mess would initiate a chain reaction in her. After several moments heaving, he went silent. Devyn studied the still form for a moment wondering if she should check for a pulse. As she inched forward he rolled over to his side and started snoring loudly.

Convinced he wasn't dead and wouldn't drown in his own vomit, she backed away. She stared at the man curled into a fetal position on the floor in a pool of his own vomit, drooling on what she assumed to be a very expensive Turkish rug, hoping Rosa would soon return. She hated to leave him alone in this condition, but clearly, she was getting no more information out of him.

He looked pathetic, nothing like the power broker she met in his office such a short time ago. In his current condition, she was no longer so certain he was involved in a deadly consortium of criminals manipulating the diet, nutrition, fitness, pharmaceutical, and medical research industries at all costs.

Rosa rushed back into the room, nudging Devyn aside. The woman gently placed the pillow under Urban's head and draped the blanket over him. She stood up and turned to Devyn. "He will be fine in the morning. Go now. I must clean him up."

Devyn nodded her head and left the house.

THIRTY-EIGHT

Sofia was having second thoughts about attending Carson's s fundraiser. Though the idea of being at the event now that he knew the truth about his father did hold some appeal. The senator acted overconfidently and cocky when he sent the invitation, certain he had nothing to fear from her presence. Divulging the horrible secret she had been carrying around for so long, tilted the tables back into her favor. She would enjoy watching him squirm.

Unfortunately, the FBI was closing in. They were circulating her photo as Candace Rogers and Janice Green. And, depending on how convincing Senator Grant was with the authorities who were inquiring about Aaron's college admission recommendation, there was a very real possibility her former mentee could lead the authorities directly to her.

As always, there would be a lot of security at the fundraiser, but none she hadn't encountered as Sofia Wilks while working in D.C. Everyone, including her, who enjoyed nearly unrestricted contact with those in the House and the Senate went through background checks. Clearly, nothing had drawn suspicion, or her access would have been questioned or revoked by now.

As long as security continued to rely on human screening at functions such as the upcoming fundraiser, she would likely remain undetected, but if facial recognition software were to be utilized, there could be trouble. Clearly this software had been used to locate Candace Rogers at the airport from photographs of Janice Green, so her disguises could not always fool the most advanced technology.

To make the decision even more complex, J.R. asked her to go and keep an eye on Terrance Yeager. Terrance was a member of Coterie, but lately his drinking and insubordination to J.R. had increased to an alarming level. J.R. was concerned that the combination of the two might loosen his tongue around the wrong people.

Like all members of Coterie, Terrance had benefitted tremendously from the organization, and more specifically, Sofia. Not only did he control a huge percentage of the exercise and weight loss CD, DVD, and print media market, she had directed a great deal of political campaign media and propaganda instigated by lobbying firms in his direction. And Coterie ensured that the market for exercise and weight loss media remained strong.

Sofia considered her options. She could refuse to go. J.R. would be disappointed, but she didn't think he would push her since Max would also be in attendance. She wasn't sure if Max and Terrance were friendly enough for Max to cover for Terrance, but that wasn't her problem. She doubted Urban would be in attendance now that Margaret was out of the picture, but if he was, that was an even bigger reason to skip the event.

Every time she convinced herself to bail, her mind returned to Carson. She wanted to observe his reaction to her presence. His response would confirm whether or not he was once again under her control or if he thought he had figured out a way to extract his family from the potential fallout that her disclosure could unleash. She hoped he would be visibly uncomfortable with her presence. She wanted him to suffer. She wanted him firmly under her thumb.

The more she thought about it the more she believed she couldn't pass up the opportunity to confirm her level of success in containing the senator and to hopefully watch him squirm. Conducting J.R.'s surveillance project couldn't hurt in order to remain in his favor should his recently pronounced love for her fade.

If she was tied to one of her former aliases, she had two ways to disappear. She could take J.R. up on his offer and go to Brazil, effectively avoiding the possibility of extradition should someone discover her whereabouts. Or if she wanted to cut her ties to J.R., she could use her recently procured identification and disguise.

Sofia stowed a go-bag with her new documents, disguise, and thirty thousand in one-hundred-dollar bills in her storage unit outside the city. If a situation ever prevented her from returning home or to the office she had an exit strategy. She would need very little time to disappear if things went wrong.

THIRTY-NINE

Devyn had arrived home to Salt Lake too late the previous night to call Gage. It was still early in the morning, but she wanted to hear his voice before heading into the office and preparing for her trip later in the day.

"Did I wake you?" she asked as Gage answered the phone.

"No. I've already fed the horses, and now I'm enjoying one last cup of coffee before heading into town. Not that it would have mattered. Wake me anytime. In fact, I'd prefer you wake me in person."

"Don't taunt me. This long-distance thing is killing me. Anyway, sorry to call so early, but I wanted to let you know I am heading out of town this afternoon and won't be home until at least Sunday."

"So, what you're saying is I should cancel the plans I made to show up unannounced to surprise you?"

"Unfortunately, yes, though my plan earlier in the week was to head north and surprise you."

Gage laughed. "As romantic as all this sounds, we better stick to clear communication and forget surprising each other. I actually was planning on sneaking to Salt Lake to visit you. Wouldn't that have been our luck to pass each other on the highway heading in different directions?"

"As much as I want to give us a chance, I'm starting to think it just isn't meant to be," Devyn said.

"I never pegged you for a quitter, Nash. So, we haven't dated in the traditional sense. We've known each other for years, though mostly through work. I've seen the tough no-nonsense side of you on the job, but I also got the chance to be with you when you're a little vulnerable. I can't even look at another woman without thinking of you. When I remember that steamy kiss you gave me on a public street in Cheyenne, well, I've definitely been wanting more ever since."

Devyn was silent for a moment. The rare tear threatened to fall. She hated all of the unfamiliar emotions he stirred in her, yet she loved feeling so alive with the possibility of a future with a wonderful man. She had convinced herself that she didn't need anyone, but if she were being honest with herself, she needed this man.

"Darn you, Harris. You are a serious complication I didn't ask for and don't need right now. My life was a lot simpler when I didn't like anyone. Now I have a girlfriend who wants to take me shopping, and you make me want to do something domestic like bake a pie."

"A pie, huh? I guess I've gotten to you as badly as you've gotten to me. I'm starting to think kids aren't that scary after all if you're with the right woman."

"This isn't funny. There's nothing worse than experiencing emotions you've never felt before and having no idea what to do about it."

"Does this mean you'll try to be patient and not give up on us yet?"

"I'm not terribly patient, but I am persistent. I almost always get what I want, and I want you."

"There's my girl. Now tell me where you're going."

Devyn told him about the senator's fundraiser, Morgan's involvement, and Nick's concern.

"I've been ordered to hide in a van down the street from the event with Gordo and Fitz so the senator isn't aware I'm in the city. Apparently, he's not my biggest fan. At least I'll be close by to back up Nick if he needs me, and hopefully, the wire on Morgan will yield something useful."

"Please be careful. Remember I've witnessed firsthand what Coterie is capable of, and if this senator is tied to the group, this assignment could be much more dangerous than it sounds."

"Believe me, I won't underestimate them again."

"Good. Call me when you can."

"I will."

"I guess I better head into town."

"Gage?"

"Yes?"

"I miss you."

"I miss you, too. You know, Devyn, I've wanted you since that counterfeiting case we worked on together all those years ago. I should have acted then instead of fumbling around looking for excuses to call you every now and then. When our paths crossed again during the Uinta Vitamin case I decided I wouldn't make the same mistake twice."

"I thought it was just lust, but I doubt the cravings last this long, so maybe we do have something," she replied.

"No doubt in my mind. Now that you agree, we just need to figure out how to make it work."

FORTY

Sofia picked up the phone and punched in the number for her in-house accountant.

"Did you process the donation I asked you to take care of last week?"

She listened to the voice on the other end, and her temper flared.

"I know it was a much larger donation than I generally make, but this organization does great work. I'm certain of the amount. Send it overnight courier today, or I'll find someone else to handle my finances."

Sofia slammed the receiver into its cradle. It infuriated her to have her motives questioned by employees. It was none of their business whom she donated money to or in what amount.

As her ire at her accountant faded, her mind wandered to Carson. A niggling warning kept telling her to stay away from his fundraiser, but she had nothing other than her gut to make her pull the plug. She trusted her instincts, but J.R.'s declaration of love had muddled her mind. She needed to bring things back into focus.

Sofia entered a number and waited. She was almost ready to hang up when a familiar voice came over the line.

"Verda?"

"Is that you, Sofia?"

"Yes, how are you doing?"

"Fine, but I am a little worried. Not that I don't enjoy hearing from you, but you haven't called in years, and now you've rang twice in as many weeks. Talk to me."

Sofia took a deep breath and remained silent for several moments wondering if she had made a mistake calling. Lately, her life seemed to be spinning out of control for the first time since becoming an adult. When Sofia was a child, Verda often made the spinning slow and occasionally, even just for a few hours after school, stop.

"After we talked last, I asked my accountant to draft a check for the center to help your after-school program. I wanted to call so you could watch out for it. You should receive the funds in a couple of days. If you don't, please call me at this number."

"I can't tell you how much the kids and I appreciate you wanting to help, but are you sure that's the only reason you called?"

"I'm thinking of taking on a new project. I may be out of the country for a while, so I probably won't be calling again."

"Something or someone exciting?"

"Possibly a bit of both. It would involve starting up a new manufacturing facility in an exotic location. There's also a man in my life, but I'm not sure how much control I'm willing to hand over to him."

"You've always had issues with trust, not that I ever blamed you. The adult that was supposed to protect you let you down, but don't allow those experiences to prevent you from achieving happiness. You deserve it."

Sofia appreciated that Verda didn't ask about what she would be manufacturing, where she would be going, or who she was seeing. Just like when she was younger, the woman went straight to the real issue at hand.

"I want to trust him, Verda. I really do."

"What's standing in the way? I hope it isn't your past still putting up roadblocks."

Sofia thought about the question for a moment.

"I'm sure it's a little of that, but I've observed many sides to him, and some are not as flattering as others."

"What is your gut telling you?"

"That I may not have a choice."

"Sofia, you are the master of your own destiny. If I taught you nothing else, I always hoped that was the one lesson that stuck."

"Until now I believed that. I thought I was in total control of my life. Lately I'm not so sure."

"How much trouble are you in? I remember you don't trust the cops, but maybe I can find someone else who can help."

"No, Verda. I shouldn't have called. I can take care of this. I'm just feeling uncharacteristically emotional."

"Love can do that to a woman."

Sofia didn't think her need to reach back into her past had anything to do with love. Maybe she was feeling a little guilty that many of the lessons Verda had tried to teach her had been a wasted effort. She taught her about strength, self-respect, independence, and hard work. Instead of using those assets to build a good life for herself, she always kept pushing for more money, more power, and revenge.

"That must be it," Sofia whispered.

"I hope so, but if it's more, promise me you'll get help. You were always too independent and proud to reach out. There are a lot of good people out there who want to do what's right, and not all police officers are bad."

"Yes. You're living proof that there are good people who want to help, but I need to take back control on my own. No one can help me undo what I've done."

"There is someone. I'll pray for you, Sofia."

Sofia bit her lip to prevent the tear from slipping down her cheek. Verda had always offered to pray for her. It was hard to have faith, but it still touched her deeply that Verda cared enough to reach out to God on her behalf.

"Thanks, Verda. I guess it couldn't hurt."

"Be careful."

"I always am. Another lesson that you taught me well."

Sofia disconnected and leaned back in her chair. Usually a conversation with Verda soothed her soul. This time the call left her more conflicted than ever. Her heart told her to give herself to J.R. Her head told her to run, and she wasn't sure which she should listen to.

FORTY-ONE

Devyn reached the office earlier than usual.

Talking to Gage always lifted her spirits, but cancelling another weekend with him for work, put her in a foul mood. She doubted Conroy would care if she asked to bail on D.C. In fact, he'd probably be relieved, but with Morgan attending the fundraiser, Devyn felt compelled to be there in case something did go wrong.

Logically there was no way Morgan could be in any danger while surrounded by so much security at the event, but when it came to Coterie, Devyn wouldn't take any chances. Simply letting Morgan drive her to the hospital in Phoenix nearly cost Morgan her life.

"So, I hear you're following Nick to D.C." Gardner stated as Devyn approached his desk on her way across the room.

Devyn kept walking, hoping something or someone would distract Gardner before the situation escalated.

"Poor guy seems to have a stalker. Every time he leaves town, Devyn goes chasing after him."

She stopped and turned to face him unable to resist the bait. "Gordo, Fitz, and I are providing support and gathering additional intel. Not my idea and I likely won't even run into him while we're there."

"I bet Nick's fiancée is getting tired of you clinging

to him. No. She's probably not too worried about a crazy woman with an imaginary boyfriend," Gardner sneered.

Devyn tried to count to ten like Nick encouraged her to do but only made it to four when she decided she no longer cared what kind of disciplinary action she'd receive for giving him a fat lip. She couldn't keep tiptoeing around him and altering her schedule to avoid him. She'd probably get suspended if she took a swing at him, but at least administrative leave would give her an opportunity to go and be with Gage at his peaceful horse property in Wyoming.

She took two steps toward him, and Gardner bolted out of his chair, clearly surprised she intended to confront him. Devyn closed half the distance between her and Gardner, fists clenched, ready for battle.

Gordo jogged up and inserted himself between her and Gardner. "Hey, Devyn, do you have a minute now to go over the equipment list we're taking with us to D.C.?"

"Can it wait?"

"No." He guided her away from Gardner. "Not only do we need to prep the gear for transport, but if you deck Gardner, Conroy probably won't let you go, and Nick will be unhappy if Conroy sends someone else."

As Devyn let the young man herd her back toward the elevator, her anger cooled. He was right, if she humiliated Gardner in front of everyone again, he would, no doubt, file a complaint against her. He was probably hoping she would take a swing at him in front of so many witnesses so she would get some sort of disciplinary action, or worse, be forced to attend anger management training.

"Thanks," Devyn said. "The satisfaction I would have gotten from wiping that smug look off his face with my fists would have been short lived. I can't let him get to me. He's not worth the effort"

"To tell you the truth, I was tempted to let it play out. He's such a jerk to the new young agents and most of the tech staff. He constantly tries to intimidate and embarrass them. There are few things I would enjoy more than watching blood spurt out of his nose. In the end, I guess I couldn't let you get in trouble for doing something we all want to do but are too afraid to try."

"Man, at times like this, I do wish I was a decade younger. You're ten times the man than Gardner ever will be."

"You're just saying that." Gordo blushed.

"I seldom say anything I don't mean."

"If things don't work out with your guy, think you'll ever consider becoming a cougar?"

"Stranger things have happened," Devyn replied as she gave him a wink and pushed the button for the elevator.

FORTY-TWO

Dusk settled over the D.C. skyline as Morgan's plane touched down. After exiting the airport, she hailed a taxi. She settled in for the long ride to the hotel where she and her friend Susan Allred had agreed to meet.

She and Susan had lost touch with each other until they recently reconnected in Sedona, Arizona. When not at her family vacation home in Sedona, Susan lived not far outside of D.C in Maryland. Morgan called, hoping for a companion to the fundraiser and was surprised that Susan not only agreed to attend, but she seemed genuinely excited by the prospect. Morgan had forgotten how politically connected Susan's family had always been, so should have expected her friend's response.

As Morgan planned, the event appeared like a fun weekend with an old friend. If she discovered nothing helpful at the fundraiser, at least she would be able to spend some time with a childhood friend and enjoy some time reminiscing about the past.

When Morgan got to the hotel, she called Susan's cell and they made plans for dinner. They chose an exclusive five-star restaurant Morgan remembered from her youth when she would come to the city with her father to attend similar functions.

Morgan quickly checked into her room, not wanting to keep Susan waiting. She freshened up, changed into more suitable attire for a high-end restaurant, and made her way to the lobby and the waiting car.

"How did you know about this place? It's fabulous," Susan asked as they perused the menu.

"My father and I used to dine here when we would come to D.C. At the time, I thought it was over-rated and pretentious, but now it brings back fond memories. I haven't always shared his political views and ambitions and neither did my mother, but it provided an opportunity to spend some time together when mother refused to accompany him."

"I understand. I would have eagerly gone to a mud wrestling event just to spend some time with either of my parents."

Morgan laughed. "You're not far off. There was always a lot of mud-slinging. Being a fashionable, seemingly-shallow teenager, the guests apparently believed I was too naïve to catch the gist of a conversation or care about what was discussed. I heard some pretty interesting and inappropriate stuff."

"Excuse me, ladies. I'm sorry to interrupt, but I have your wine. Would you like to examine it first?"

Morgan and Susan looked at each other. Both shook their heads, indicating they trusted the choice and motioned for the waiter to pour. After he served the wine and took their orders he left them once again in privacy.

"So, why return to the ring now?"

"Now that Nick and I are back together, I've decided to take some time off work. I've dedicated my life to my own success, and it nearly cost me everything, at least everything that mattered. I'm going to try new things while I have this opportunity. I've started painting again, and I'm taking an art class at a nearby college. I'm volunteering at the food pantry and I'm trying to catch up on politics. These may all be passing interests, but I want to see what I've been missing."

Morgan hated to lie to her friend, but at least it was only a partial untruth. She had taken up painting again, enrolled in an art class at the college, and was volunteering two afternoons a week with the local food pantry. She had no desire to get involved with politics to the level her father had been, but she figured it wouldn't hurt to at least be a little more informed.

"I remember when we were younger and our families would spend a few months each summer in Sedona. You shared with me some amazing oils you painted of the stunning landscapes in the area. I was always amazed at your talent and was surprised the summer before our junior year in high school when you abruptly quit."

"My parents weren't a big fan of the arts. I was reminded that few can make a lot of money by painting pretty pictures."

"At least your parents thought you were capable of succeeding in business. I was actually encouraged in the arts since I was expected to do like generations of women before in my family and marry well and possess all the cultured skills necessary for entertaining."

"Well then, we'll make a good team at the fundraiser tomorrow night. If the stock market comes up, I'll bore everyone to death, and you can be in charge of keeping me from committing some dreadful social faux pas."

"Here's to a great partnership," Susan stated as

she raised her glass.

"And to renewing old friendships," Morgan replied as she tapped her glass to Susan's. "My career didn't allow much time for socializing or making new friends, so it's nice to reconnect with a good friend from simpler times."

After a three hour, five-course dinner, and ample amounts of wine the two women made their way back to the hotel. As much as Morgan enjoyed Susan's company and talking about old times, she enjoyed eating pizza and cookie dough with Devyn even more.

Morgan didn't understand why Devyn got such a bad rap with her co-workers. She was a lot of fun, possessed a good heart, and her insecurities about men were endearing. Morgan couldn't believe that Devyn had no idea she was a knockout.

Exiting the limousine that the hotel had sent to fetch them, Morgan struggled to avoid looking around for Devyn. She wasn't sure if she was even in D.C. yet or where she was staying. She doubted Nick was watching her from the shadows since he was attached to a security detail, but at least he was nearby. Knowing Devyn was there or on the way and Nick was close gave Morgan a sense of relief and dread—relief that she wasn't alone, dread that she might need their protection.

After planning how they would spend the next day in the city, Morgan said good night to Susan. She hurried to her room, anxious to be secured behind a deadbolt on a secure floor, but mostly just anxious to talk to Nick. She couldn't believe how much she missed him after being apart for only three days. She was even more surprised at how nervous she felt with her involvement in trying to gather information about the senator. She couldn't imagine there could possibly be any connection between him and Coterie, but if there were, he could be dangerous.

When she volunteered to Special Agent In Charge, Gerald Conroy, she believed she was simply going to a party to mingle and listen. What harm could come of that? She tried to convince herself that the nightmare in Phoenix was behind her, but now it came flooding back in a terrifying torrent—bound, gagged, waking up in a pitch-black semi-trailer, disoriented and fearing the person who opened the door might kill her.

FORTY-THREE

Devyn was relieved when she learned they would be flying from Salt Lake City to Washington D.C. in one of the agency's private planes. Gordo and Fitz insisted on taking their own surveillance equipment, and Conroy agreed, so it proved the best option.

His boss in the national office was the only one in the FBI aware of Devyn, Gordo, and Fitz's involvement, so borrowing what they needed from the local office was out. Besides, Gordo and Fitz were more comfortable with their own gear, and flying commercial with weapons and other high-tech electronics wasn't easy.

Conroy convinced his boss that allowing Devyn to monitor the operation was a good idea since she was more likely to recognize Candace Rogers or Janice Green than anyone else if the woman known by both names happened to show up. They doubted she would, but if she and Senator Grant were both involved in Coterie, the possibility existed. Devyn's small team was also the only ones who would be specifically watching Morgan since no one locally was aware of her true reason for being at the fundraiser.

Her phone display read nearly midnight when they finally touched down at a private airstrip outside the city. Devyn hoped to arrive hours earlier, but it had taken longer than anticipated to load the jet and get all the paperwork in order.

The thought of leaving Morgan unprotected for so long made her uncomfortable. There was no reason to believe Morgan was in danger, but Devyn had no desire to gamble with her best friend's safety or experience a repeat of Phoenix.

As promised, a non-descript rental van was waiting for their arrival. They quickly transferred all their equipment and weapons from the plane into the van and headed into the city. The hotel where they planned to stay was located a block away from Morgan's hotel. With increasing doubts about the safety of Morgan's involvement with what appeared on the surface to be a typical fundraiser, a block away seemed like a hundred miles.

Devyn quickly checked her messages to make sure she hadn't missed any calls from Nick or Morgan while in flight. Confident everything was quiet in D.C., she called Conroy to let him know they had arrived and were en route to the hotel. Despite being late, her boss appreciated the status update and was clearly waiting for the call.

"Any movement on any fronts?" Gordo asked.

"No," she replied.

"I'd say that's good news."

Devyn nodded but couldn't shake the feeling that this whole operation was a bad idea. There should be plenty of security, including Nick, yet the whole thing set off warning bells in Devyn's head.

"Nick didn't blame you for what happened in Arizona," Gordo said.

"How can you possibly know that?" Devyn asked.

"He told me."

"Really? Nick, the man who confides in no one, told you he didn't blame me for almost getting Morgan killed in Arizona?"

"Well, not in so many words. I asked him when you were coming back to work and he said when your ribs healed enough for you to get around without help and when you quit beating yourself up for something that wasn't your fault."

"Maybe he meant for letting our best shot at getting answers die," she said.

"No. I think he was talking about Morgan because he then mumbled something about her being the only woman he knew more stubborn than you. If he couldn't bend her to his will, how could he expect you to do it after a brief meeting?"

Devyn reached over and slugged Gordo, making the van swerve as he tried to absorb her punch while driving.

"Why didn't you say something before now? I've relived that nightmare over and over a million times. You could have spared me dozens of sleepless nights."

"I was saving it for our first date," Gordo yanked back as if she might hit him again.

Devyn couldn't help herself. She wanted to be mad, but a smile crept across her lips. "Darn. Sometimes I really wish I was ten years younger."

"I'm four years older than Gordo," Fitz chimed in from the back seat.

"Don't even go there. I still got dibs if the sheriff thing doesn't pan out," Gordo warned, while briefly glowering at Fitz in the review mirror.

"Yep, sorry Fitz, if I decide to go the cougar route, I've already found my cub." Devyn ruffled Gordo's hair.

"I figured I'd eventually wear her down. Unfortunately, I was too late to beat some tough guy sheriff to the punch," Gordo mumbled as he returned his focus to driving.

As the van eased off at the exit that would lead them to a much-needed bed at the downtown hotel, Devyn exhaled a sigh of relief. If anything was going down Nick would have called. In a few minutes she'd be within a block of Morgan should anything go wrong.

FORTY-FOUR

The phone in Morgan's room rang. She was running a bit late since it took Devyn more time than anticipated to get the surveillance wire in place under Morgan's elegant evening gown.

"Hey, Susan, sorry I'm so slow. I'm almost ready. I'll meet you in the lobby in five minutes."

"No hurry. We do want to be fashionably late," Susan replied. "I'll call for a car, and it should be here by the time you get down to the lobby."

Morgan was so nervous that she was having a difficult time getting her hair and makeup just right. She wished Devyn hadn't already left. Devyn often made her laugh unintentionally, and she could use some humor at the moment. Morgan had made light of her participation in the operation to Nick and Devyn, but if she were being honest with herself she was absolutely terrified.

Acting wasn't in her repertoire, so she hoped she could pull off the character she needed to play. Tonight, Morgan Hunter was a single, wealthy, politically active woman out on the town with her long-time friend and not opposed to the attention of possible suitors. When, in actuality, she hated politics and was so in love with Nick she wasn't sure she could flirt with the senator or anyone else if the opportunity arose. It would be difficult to avoid spending the entire evening looking for Nick in the room, despite being strictly instructed to stifle any impulse to find him.

With one last look in the mirror, Morgan decided she had done all she could, and there was no point in delaying any longer. Inhaling a deep breath, she excited her room, entered the elevator and then pushed the down arrow.

"Stunning," Susan stated as Morgan approached her in the lobby.

"But not as gorgeous as you," Morgan replied with the calmest smile she could muster while her stomach did summersaults.

"All in all, not bad for two women no longer in their twenties,"

Morgan laughed, "That's an understatement. We're barely hanging on to our thirties."

The ride to the hotel hosting the fundraiser went quickly. All the banter with Susan about summers in Sedona when they were kids and rehashing their shopping and sightseeing adventures earlier in the day helped Morgan push the thoughts about the real reason she was attending the function out of her mind and focus on her mission.

Once inside the banquet hall with the other attendees, she needed to be alert and take in every detail. If she didn't get some useful information a lot of time, effort, and money would go to waste. Mostly, she didn't want to let Nick, Devyn, and Agent Conroy down.

They pulled up in front of the hotel, and a young impeccably dressed young man opened their door and greeted them. "I assume you're here for the fundraiser?" he asked.

"Yes," Morgan replied.

"Follow me please."

The polite staffer escorted Morgan and Susan into the hotel and left them at the reception desk where their invitation and identification were verified. Susan's family was wealthier and much more politically connected than Morgan's, so bringing Susan along had been a good move.

They were immediately directed into the main banquet hall and told they would be sitting at the senator's table. When Morgan reached for a glass of wine on a passing waiter's tray, she was stopped and informed her drink was on its way and they would be assigned a private waiter for the evening to ensure all their needs were promptly met.

All the pomp brought back memories from Morgan's childhood and she was more certain than ever she had no desire to resume that lifestyle. Nick would be uncomfortable with her tapping into her trust fund, and she was OK with leaving it untouched. She was perfectly happy to live within Nick's means if it meant being together, a lesson she had almost learned too late.

Morgan accepted a wine glass from the special waiter assigned to cater to specific guests. She smiled and thanked him. As she looked up to scan the crowd her gaze locked on Senator Grant. He had clearly been watching her. He looked away and whispered to a young woman whom Morgan assumed was a staffer since she wore a discrete headset and was dressed in professional attire as opposed to formal.

The young woman disappeared into the crowd, and Morgan lost sight of her. She continued to peruse the room in the off chance she might still recognize some of the political power-players from her father's generation. A few elderly men looked vaguely familiar, but she wasn't certain enough of anyone's identity to risk introducing herself to any of the gentlemen.

As she turned toward Susan, the same woman who had been at the senator's side moments earlier approached them.

"Ms. Hunter, Ms. Allred, I'm Carolyn Fields, Senator Grant's assistant. Please follow me, and I'll introduce you to the senator."

Morgan and Susan exchanged looks, shrugged their shoulders, and followed as instructed.

~*~

"Wow, that didn't take long. If Nick heard I bet he's grinding his teeth thinking about Morgan chumming up with the senator," Devyn said to Gordo and Fitz.

"He won't catch any of this. Conroy didn't want him having a live feed for fear he'd get distracted. Morgan's all ours for now," Gordo replied.

"That's why he's the boss," Devyn mumbled. "Fitz, how many cameras are up and running?"

"Only two, one in Morgan's broach and one on a statue in the corner that gives a decent panorama of the room. We didn't have the time or resources to do more with the security detail keeping such a close eye on things. If it wasn't for Nick's covert installation the only eyes we'd have on the party would be courtesy of Morgan."

Devyn was glad the van was too small for her to pace, or she'd be rocking the vehicle with her nervous energy. She stood hunched over behind Fitz and looked at the two monitors. With Morgan following behind Ms. Fields, all they could see was the young woman's back, and the other camera yielded nothing else helpful.

She returned her attention to Gordo, who was tapping away at a keyboard trying to enhance the audio feed so the sound would come through more clearly.

"Is that as good as it gets?" Devyn asked.

"It's difficult to get good audio when there's so much going on, but it's all being recorded so when we get back to the lab we can clean it up and isolate anything significant," Gordo replied.

"Well that doesn't do a lot of good right here, right now. I hope we can understand Morgan if she needs help."

"Don't worry, everything's being simultaneously fed through the computer and searched for key words. I'll make sure 'help' is one of those words," Gordo joked.

"Sorry. I hate being stuck in this claustrophobic tin can while my only link to the outside is through a garbled mic and a tiny camera."

"Welcome to our world," Fitz added. "This is about as exciting as it gets."

FORTY-FIVE

The cab pulled up in front of the hotel. The unloading zone buzzed with activity. Sofia gazed around, quickly identifying the plain clothes private security, hotel staff, and police officers providing security outside the building. They were easy to spot despite their attempts to blend in. Their presence made her nervous, though there were far fewer personnel than she would have expected considering the guest list.

"That'll be thirty-two bucks," the driver stated, interrupting her thoughts.

She thought about asking him to take her back home, but she was compelled to observe the scene for herself, keep an eye on Terrance as J.R. requested, and gauge Senator Grant's reaction to her presence.

Digging through her purse, she pulled two twenties out of her wallet and handed the bills to the impatient cabbie. Before she could exit the vehicle, a young, well-dressed man opened the door and extended his hand. She placed her hand in his and let him escort her up the small flight of steps to the grand entry of the hotel.

"I assume you're here for the fundraiser?"

Sofia nodded.

"Once inside, you'll need to show your invitation and identification to that woman," he said pointing to a woman holding a computer tablet standing near a reception desk next to the banquet hall door off to their right. "Thank you for coming and enjoy your evening."

She thanked the man and followed his directions. The woman guarding the entrance to the event barely glanced at her or her ID, not that it mattered since Sofia was attending as herself. A steady stream of invitees entered the hotel lobby and converged upon the woman at the door, forcing her to do only a cursory glance at identifications and invitations.

As Sofia passed through the large double doors a waiter handed her a glass of wine. She accepted the glass and found a spot at the back of the room near a decorative column where she could watch the crowd without drawing attention.

From her vantage point she could observe nearly everyone entering the room and anyone approaching the bar for something stronger than the wine being carried on trays and doled out to guests by efficient waitstaff. The room was too large and too crowded to see the tables near the front, but those people would sooner or later wander by as they worked the room as they always did. The main reason most of the invitees attended these functions was to be seen by a certain social group: those with money and power.

Sofia recognized nearly everyone. In her line of work it was important to be familiar with as many of the politicians and their staffers as possible. She recognized reporters, other lobbyist, the usual litany of high-dollar campaign donors, successful business professionals, and other players in the elite D.C. social scene.

To avoid drawing attention Sofia slowly left her perch and mingled with the large crowd. Most were so busy trying to impress each other that few paid her any notice as she worked her way around the room.

"Sofia, surprised to see you here," Max Markis stated. "I hope J.R. didn't send you to keep an eye on me."

"Not you."

"Terrance making him nervous?"

"His insolence and excessive drinking are a cause for concern."

Max motioned to a waiter heading in their direction. He snagged two glasses of wine off of the tray and handed one to Sofia.

She watched him during his distraction. He was an interesting man with many facets. The last time she saw him in Florida he blended in well with the other businessmen in town for meetings or a weekend of golf.

When they were last alone together, he was helping her make a hasty retreat from Arizona in his small private aircraft. His face had revealed a two-day growth of beard, his longish light brown hair had been secured in a band at the nape of his neck, and he had worn a torn and stained t-shirt and jeans. His look then could be described as little else but dangerous, but he cleaned up well. Tonight, he portrayed the perfect successful businessman at home in this high-dollar, socially elite scene.

"Are you sure it's a good idea to be here? I thought you might lay low for a while," Max asked.

"No one has ever tied me to one of my aliases. I work with most of these people on a regular basis so my attendance is nothing out of the ordinary. Aside from J.R.'s concern over Terrance's loyalty, I believe I took care of my difficulties with the senator, but I wanted to find out if I was completely successful."

"Speak of the devil," Max whispered.

"Sofia, so glad you decided to join us. You are looking lovely as always."

Sofia locked eyes with Carson but said nothing. She was pleased to observe the twitch at the corner of his right eye and the way he licked his lips repeatedly. He was clearly nervous by her presence. He forced a smile and turned his attention to Max.

"Mr. Markis, I'm honored you came. I always love chatting with the businessmen and women who are out in the trenches creating jobs, bolstering the economy, and living the American dream. As you are well aware, I'm very pro-business and a good ally for anyone in business."

"A pleasure as always, Senator. Thanks for the invitation. I'm sure it will be a very interesting evening. And enough of these, and I'll probably be pulling out my checkbook by the end of the night." Max held up his glass.

"Well in that case, waiter, keep this man's hands full." Carson laughed as he flagged down a server, slapped Max on the back, and moved on.

Neither said a word until Carson was engaged in conversation with another potential donor.

"Well?" Max asked. "He seemed a bit on edge to me."

"Yes, I'm confident he'll continue to do our bidding with no more hesitancy."

"I'd sure love to know what you're holding over him. It must be good. Many politicians are so immoral nowadays that an extra-marital affair or a little dirty business dealing wouldn't be enough for you to exert such control."

Sofia ignored Max's comment. Her mind

wandered back twenty years and a flood of memories came rushing in. She had ensured Carson's loyalty, but she wasn't sure she could continue the game. She spent years building a wall around her heart to block the guilt and pain. Between J.R.'s declaration of love and having to relive her mother's murder, she felt those carefully constructed walls crumbling down around her.

"You OK?"

"What?"

"I've been talking, and you clearly haven't heard a word I've said. You're a million miles away. What gives?" Max asked as he wiped a tear from her cheek with his thumb.

"I'm sorry. I shouldn't have come. It was a bad idea. Too many ugly secrets lurk in the shadows of places like this."

"Speaking of ugly secrets, look who just walked in?"

Sofia was thankful Max didn't press and that he offered her an out. She glanced at the doorway.

"Another one I'll never understand why J.R. let in," Sofia mumbled. "He's nearly as weak as Preston was."

"This can't be good," Max stated.

Sofia agreed, but she wasn't sure what to do about it. Word was that Urban totally collapsed with the news of Margaret's death and hadn't been sober since he received the news.

"Should I call J.R.?" Max asked.

Sofia thought for a moment. She wasn't sure how Urban would react to her. Would he think she played some role in his wife's death?

"No, I'll do it. Keep an eye on him. He may not be

happy to see me, or worse, I may be the reason he came."

She turned to leave but was stopped abruptly by Max's iron grip on her upper arm.

"Look in my eyes and tell me the truth, Sofia. Did you kill Margaret, or do you know for sure she was murdered?"

The fact that another human being would ask her that question made her realize how morally and ethically low she had sunk in life. She had gone through childhood and her early adult life with no one thinking she was capable of anything. Now people found her capable of murder, which sadly, she was.

"No. I didn't touch Margaret, and I know nothing for sure, but I have my suspicions. I'd been begging J.R. to get rid of Trevor with no luck, but the day before Margaret's death, he disappeared and I haven't seen him since. Well, not officially. I did catch a glimpse of him in disguise, stalking me outside my office well after Margaret's passing."

Max shook his head. "This is not what I signed up for. I wanted to make a lot money, bend the markets to my will, and make a few chosen people sweat. These recent deaths are hitting too close to home. What's to guarantee I'm not next?"

"I doubt you will believe this, but I agree. I loved the game, the money, punishing those in my past who deserved to pay for their transgressions, but I never dreamed it would go this far. The losses of Justine and Aaron have been very difficult for me. Unfortunately, I doubt any of us are free to break ties with Coterie and walk away even if we wanted to. Keep an eye on Urban, and I'll go call J.R."

Sofia slipped out of the room and entered the main

hotel lobby. It was crawling with security, but there were plenty of other guests not affiliated with the event milling around, enabling her to blend in with the crowd. She found a dimly lit quiet corner and dialed J.R.'s number.

After a quick exchange, she walked over to the bar and ordered a double scotch. She seldom drank hard liquor, but she needed something to calm her nerves. She raised the glass to her lips and threw the caramel-colored liquid back in one gulp, hoping Urban wasn't currently doing the same.

FORTY-SIX

Morgan felt like a circus novelty. Apparently, these events were usually attended by the same group of people, and a new face in the crowd drew attention. Susan wasn't a stranger to these type of functions and was familiar with many of the players. Susan introduced her to so many politicians, socialites, and business men and women that Morgan's head was spinning. Luckily, she didn't need to try and remember all the names since every word spoken within four feet of her was being recorded in some discrete van parked along the street.

"It truly is a pleasant surprise to see a new face at one of these events, and what a lovely face it is. Pardon me for saying so. This may be an enjoyable evening after all."

Smiling, she accepted the compliment from the seventy-year-old business mogul, wishing he would take a step away and remove his hand from her back.

"Not that new," Senator Grant interrupted. "Her father, Charles Hunter, was a generous contributor to my father's campaigns. I'm hoping to carry a mutually rewarding relationship on to a new generation."

"Charles Hunter, well I remember him. Why haven't we seen you around here before?" the old man asked.

"I've buried myself in my work. Recently I've reassessed my priorities and decided to get back to some of the more important things in life."

"Nothing's more important than being involved in the political processes," Senator Grant added. "Now, if you'll excuse us, we're about ready to get the call to be seated for dinner, and I noticed this lovely lady is seated at my table."

Morgan was having a difficult time picturing the senator as the enemy after he rescued her from an overly friendly gentleman from her father's era. So far, he had been nothing but polite and charming.

"I hope you'll forgive him. He is quite harmless, but it's been awhile since all of the old regulars have seen a woman so enchanting."

"Thank you for the compliment and for rescuing me. I didn't want to hurt his feelings. I was taught to respect my elders," Morgan replied, hoping she had only thought about rolling her eyes and didn't actually do it in response to his flattery.

Senator Grant laughed. "I won't tell him you referred to him as your 'elder,' or it would crush his ego. He still considers himself a lady's man."

As they stood near the main table at the front of the banquet hall Morgan glanced down and noticed that the place cards indicated she was seated between Susan and the senator. She looked around, wishing Susan hadn't deserted her but realizing she should take advantage of this rare opportunity to be alone with the senator.

"Did you know my father personally?"

"I don't recall ever meeting him, but my father recognized the name and said Charles Hunter was a great man, an even better businessman, and a champion of the free market and the American dream."

Morgan smiled. He was definitely a polished schmoozer.

"I'm probably a little biased, but yes, he was a great man and very good at realizing that dream. I've decided recently that it's time to take what he taught me and put it to better use. I've left the corporate world, and I plan to put my energies into investing more seriously."

"Hence the renewed interest in politics?"

She smiled. "Father always said it's imperative to have absolute confidence that those in power won't throw you a curveball when you least expect it. Your voting record mirrors your father's. I would think two generations of predictable support gives an investor that sense of security."

"Are there opportunities you're particularly interested in pursuing?" he asked. "I'm here to serve my constituents and the American voters in any capacity I can."

"In my rebellious, 'I'll make my own way,' youth, I took a position as a pharmaceutical rep. I then worked my way up in the company before moving on to other corporate ventures. I learned a lot in those early years. I have yet to work in an industry that realizes the same profit margins as pharmaceuticals. So, to answer your question, yes, I'm planning to expand my investment portfolio to include a larger percentage of medical research and pharmaceutical stocks."

The smile that had been etched on the senator's face since he approached her sagged. The pause before he spoke was definable.

"Always a good bet there. Now if you'll excuse me, I better go retrieve my parents since I spotted the emcee heading toward the podium to no doubt ask everyone to be seated so the waitstaff can start serving dinner. Oh, and here's Ms. Allred to keep you company."

Susan was all smiles when she approached Morgan. She grabbed her hand and leaned in close to whisper in Morgan's ear.

"It's no wonder Edward doesn't like me coming to these events without him. I may be a little rusty at recognizing the signs, but I think I've been propositioned three times already."

"I must not be doing something right, I've only received two, and I'm not even married," Morgan replied.

"Thank you for calling and inviting me along. This is doing my self-esteem a world of good."

"Glad I could help, but your self-esteem shouldn't need a boost. You're still as beautiful as ever, you're married to a wonderful man, and the two of you have obviously taken very good care of the family legacy."

"Thank you. I'm grateful for all I have, but when a woman reaches a certain age, it's flattering to learn she can still turn a few heads."

"No worries, you're definitely turning more than a few. Now let's take our seats before we get scolded. The senator's staff is clearly getting a little frustrated with trying to keep the program moving."

With one last casual glance around the room for Nick, Morgan took her seat, hoping she hadn't already blown it with the senator.

FORTY-SEVEN

The tiny camera in the broach on Morgan's lapel was pretty much worthless. Devyn could hear all Morgan's conversations, but until Morgan talked to someone a good foot shorter all they were going to observe was a fine collection of neckties or more cleavage than she cared to look at.

When Morgan brought up the pharmaceutical industry the senator had definitely paused and changed gears, but without his expression and body language, it was difficult to interpret the reason. So far, all they had captured were enough men hitting on Nick's ex-wife, soon-to-be-wife again, to send him over the edge when he listened to the audio feed.

Devyn picked up her phone and dialed her partner.

"Anything interesting?"

"Not as far as my colleagues are concerned, but Urban Blair showed up alone," Nick replied.

"That is odd. The last time I saw him he was passed out on the floor of his living room in a pool of his own vomit crying around about 'jars sofa mess.' I couldn't understand if he spilled a jar of preserves on the couch or if the words I heard weren't the words he was trying to say."

"How's Morgan doing?"

"Fine. So far all we've got is a bunch of boring stuffy party chitchat. It's early, so, hopefully, people will loosen up after a few more drinks."

Devyn saw no point in taunting Nick with any of Morgan's propositions. She'd save that for another day when she was bored and needed some lively entertainment.

"I hope she doesn't ask the wrong questions, or I guess, for that matter, the right questions," Nick mumbled.

"She'll be fine. Let me know if you get eyes on Urban. I'd love to find out who he's associating with. The lapel camera is a bust, literally. That's about all we can see. With so many people milling around the one camera you managed to sneak in for us, the video feed is pretty much a blur of black suits and diamonds. I'd kill to get a peek at what's going on in there."

"I can see Morgan most of the time since there's a camera focused directly on the senator's table, but so far Urban's been a ghost. All I know is that he checked in. The list of attendees is constantly updated in case anyone on our watch list shows up," Nick replied. "Gotta go. Keep me posted."

"Will do."

Devyn stood as straight as she could in the back of the van and tried to stretch her stiff back. Her muscles cramped and she was plagued by claustrophobia. Something didn't feel right, but she couldn't put her finger on it and being so immobile and far from the action, only made her anxiety worse.

"Gordo, your mom didn't happen to stash a batch of cinnamon rolls or brownies in your gear, did she?"

"Nope. Sorry. I didn't tell her what I was doing or who I was going with."

"She only bakes for you," Fitz added as he rolled his eyes.

"Well, I'm starving. I'm going for some food," Devyn stated as she stuck a tiny bud in her ear. "Test me, Gordo."

"Still dating the sheriff," he whispered into his mic.

Devyn slugged his shoulder playfully.

"I'll take that as a yes to both inquiries."

"Anything special either of you want?" she asked as she checked her weapon out of habit and stowed in the back of her jeans under her leather jacket.

"A couple cups of good, hot, strong coffee and something sweet would help," Gordo stated. "I take mine black and you'd better grab some cream for my sidekick."

"Sidekick? Like you're some kind of super hero," Fitz mumbled.

Devyn couldn't help but smile. The two techs had wormed their way into her heart. Even though she felt too old to date either, she still enjoyed working with them and respected the skills they brought to the table. She was amazed at what they could accomplish through the Internet, hi-tech electronics, and other digital means. She could barely check her e-mail.

"I'll be back in a few. Keep me posted. If anyone so much as sneezes around Morgan, I want to know. Also, pull up a photo of Urban Blair and see if you can locate him in the crowd. We need to identify everyone he's hanging with."

"You got it," Gordo replied.

Devyn slipped out of the van. No one noticed her as she joined the small group of pedestrians on the sidewalk. She tried to stroll casually as the flow headed in the direction of the hotel. The nighttime temperatures were pleasant, the street lights provided ample illumination, and not a single siren wailed in the city. There was nothing to cause alarm except for her gut.

Glancing around, she took an inventory of the security near the hotel. She spotted no snipers on any roofs and all of the agents and officers seemed concentrated around the main entrance. She hoped every door in and out of the building was covered, but she had her doubts.

Nick reported that there wasn't as many personnel assigned as usual because no one considered the senator or any of his guests to be especially high-risk targets. The senator traveled with his usual security detail and additional local law enforcement was added due to a few fairly well-off guests. The additional officers were primarily at the front entrance of the building. The hotel provided extra security for the event as well, but nothing extraordinary.

If Senator Grant was involved with Coterie as Devyn suspected, she hoped this evening would remain strictly social. Any confrontation with Coterie and she feared the security detail would be grossly under-prepared.

FORTY-EIGHT

Sofia sat at a table near the back of the room with five other lobbyists she recognized and a wealthy couple from Illinois, who had flown in from the senator's home state for the function. She purposely took a seat with her back to the wall so she could observe guests making their way to the front of the banquet hall.

A sharply dressed middle-aged emcee approached the podium and tapped on the microphone. "Could I have everyone's attention. If you will all take your seats the waitstaff will be serving dinner, and please keep the space between the tables clear. Thank you."

Sofia felt a little guilty leaving Max to babysit Urban, but Max agreed it was for the best. Once she relayed her conversation with J.R. to Max that Trevor was nearby should any problems arise, they wanted to make certain Urban didn't cause a scene. The fact that Trevor was lurking in the shadows didn't make either one of them more comfortable, but rather increasingly on edge.

Max reported that the first question Urban asked was if she was in attendance, which added to her desire to avoid him. Confronting her about any role she played in his wife's death was the only reason Sofia could imagine he would come to an event he claimed to dislike while grieving for his recently departed wife.

Assuming Max could keep Urban away from her and under control, Sofia focused on J.R.'s other concern. Her current seat selection put her close enough to listen to Terrance Yeager's conversations at his table next to hers. So far, he had drunk in moderation and kept conversations to business and politics.

Even though Santa Fe law enforcement remained silent on whether they suspected any foul play in Margaret's death. Anyone close to J.R. would likely consider the possibility. Sofia couldn't help but wonder if, after Margaret's death, Terrence decided it might be best to quit pushing J.R.'s buttons.

As Carson approached her table, Sofia's gaze locked on his. He was trailed closely by an elderly couple whom she recognized as his parents. The short, slightly hunched over white-haired woman looked so frail that Sofia could summon up no dislike, only pity, for the woman who was not directly involved in her disastrous childhood.

Carson stopped to shake hands with the couple from Illinois. He slowly made his way around the table to shake each person's hand, saving Sofia until last. He took her hand and shook it like the rest of the guests then leaned in close to her ear and whispered, "Polk Genetic Research filed for a patent on their procedure to isolate a gene that may contribute to genetic obesity. Apparently, the scientist who allegedly committed suicide didn't code his notes that well after all."

Sofia stared at him in disbelief for a brief moment, unable to respond. As her focus returned, she slowly angled her head so no one else at the table could hear her response.

"Why are you telling me this?"

"Thought you might be interested. Thank you for coming," he added, louder than the first comment for those who might be listening.

Sofia tried not to stare as he moved on. What did he know? Was he just connecting the dots, or did he learn something to level the playing field? There was no way he could know Coterie was responsible for keeping the scientist's work from going public. The assassin who had completed that job left no clues and he was now dead.

The Polk Genetic Research job had been Coterie's second operation executed to manipulate the market. When they learned of the game-changing scientific breakthrough, they had reacted quickly and decisively. The group had taken some pretty drastic measures in the early years to ensure the American people needed the diet and nutrition products they were producing, manufacturing, and selling, and everyone in the group got rich or richer.

Sofia tried to shake off the exchange. As she looked up and refocused on the activity around her she caught Carson's father's eye. George Grant looked over at her and smiled. She saw no recognition in his eyes, which didn't surprise her. He hadn't seen her since she was fifteen. He hadn't changed much over the years. His hair was a little grayer, and he packed around a few more pounds, but she would have recognized him anywhere.

He reached into his pocket, and Sofia's gaze froze on his hand. She held her breath as he slowly removed a slender object. She exhaled – a pen, not a syringe. Her pulse raced as visions flooded her mind in an overpowering rush, making her dizzy. Her mouth went dry and her ears rang. She reached for her water and took a long sip.

"Are you OK?" a fellow lobbyist asked.

"I'm feeling a little flush. Please excuse me."

Sofia pushed back from her chair, thankful Carson and his family had moved on. The encounters with the elder and younger senator caused her world to spin wildly out of control. Her past just collided with her future in a matter of seconds. She needed to think and rein in her emotions in order to get through the rest of the evening. Her life might depend on the decisions she made in the next few minutes.

Walking as calmly as possible on shaky legs until she was out of the room, Sofia practiced the breathing techniques Verda had taught her while studying martial arts as a child. Soon her equilibrium slowly began to return.

Once out of sight of the woman manning the door to keep out uninvited guests, she turned the corner into an empty hallway leading to the ladies' room and hastened her pace. Relieved to be away from the crowd, she pushed through the restroom door, stepped into the furthest stall, and locked the door. Closing her eyes, she continued her breathing exercises until her pulse slowed and the image of the elder Senator Grant holding a needle over her mother's lifeless body faded.

FORTY-NINE

Senator Grant exuded the charm and charisma of a seasoned politician. He pandered to everyone who wasn't related to him but paid Morgan no special attention. She didn't know if he was simply behaving in front of his parents and wife or if she had struck a nerve with her comment about wanting to invest in pharmaceuticals and medical research. She feared she had gotten all the information she was going to and Nick, Devyn, and Agent Conroy would be disappointed at the waste of time and money.

As the guests dined on the elegantly prepared meal, the senator went to the podium and gave a speech about his accomplishments, what he hoped to accomplish if re-elected, and how much he needed everyone's support to ensure he could continue to represent the business segment of the population constantly under attack by what he called "the bleeding-heart liberals."

Morgan applauded his political savvy. His comments about the previous administration and how much work he and his colleagues undertook to reverse old policies drew lots of grumbling and head nods. She had no doubt the donations would pour in after his oration.

"Again, thank you all for coming tonight. Thank you for your continued support, and please stay and enjoy the wonderful band that will be playing for us this evening. Eat up, drink up, dance, and I hope to see you all on the campaign trail."

Back at the table, the senator's wife, Elizabeth, was all smiles as she greeted him with a proper kiss on the cheek. Morgan stifled a laugh as his mother told him what a wonderful job he did. Apparently, even senior politicians still received praise from their mothers.

"Shall we get this started, Elizabeth," Senator Grant said as he took his wife's hand and escorted her onto the dance floor.

Before long, an elderly gentleman coaxed Susan onto the dance floor and the other couples at the table joined in except for the senator's parents.

"So, you're Charles's daughter? He was a great supporter of mine for many years," George Grant stated.

"He believed you were looking out for the interests of big business. I've spent my career in upper management of some of the largest corporations in the country, so I understand how important it is to have an ally in Washington. Your son shares those same values, and I decided it was time to get more involved."

"Unfortunately, they share too many of the same values," George's wife mumbled.

"That's enough, Rosalyn. Ms. Hunter doesn't want to hear about your son's or your husband's faults. She is quite stunning, so she'll likely discover some of those on her own if she hangs around this group long enough."

"Actually, I'm sure a mother's prospective would be quite entertaining," Morgan replied with a little smile that she hoped would put the elder Grants at ease.

As the band paused, some couples remained on

the floor. The senator cut in with Susan and the senator's wife, Elizabeth, returned to the table to escort her father-in-law onto the dance floor.

"My hip is too stiff to dance, so it's nice Elizabeth helps to keep him entertained rather than leaving him to rely on his own judgement," Roslyn said. "I'm surprised you haven't been dragged out onto the floor yet."

"Well it's only been two songs and we are tucked away here in the front of the room. To be perfectly honest, though, it won't disappoint me a bit if I'm overlooked. I didn't come here looking for a date. I'm simply interested in the senator's message. I want to make an informed decision about whether or not I continue to support his campaign."

"Smart woman," Mrs. Grant stated.

"He seems like a very honest man with a high degree of integrity. Integrity and strong moral values are some of the traits my father admired most in your husband while he was serving," Morgan stated, hoping she hadn't laid on the exaggerated praise too thickly.

Rosalyn started coughing. She tapped lightly at her chest with her fingertips and shook her head.

Nervous that the old woman was choking, Morgan raced around the table and sat next to the senator's mother.

"Are you OK?" Morgan handed Rosalyn her glass of water.

The old woman nodded, accepted the glass in Morgan's hand, and took a sip.

"Would you like me to get your husband or a staffer?"

"No, dear. I'll be fine."

"Are you sure?"

"Yes. You seem like a very nice woman with good family values. I love my son and he's a good politician. I encourage you to donate to his campaign because he will look out for your business interests, but be careful not to give him even the slightest encouragement. Please."

"Excuse me?"

"He does take after his father in more ways than his political values and sometimes that comes back to cause the family unnecessary difficulties. Elizabeth is a tad boring, but she's been very patient and tolerant, and I would hate to see her publicly humiliated by my son's extracurricular activities."

"Since mother doesn't dance there is only one lovely lady left at this table I hope will do me the honor," Senator Grant stated as he extended a hand toward Morgan.

Morgan looked at Rosalyn. The old woman nodded her head once and picked up her water glass. Not wanting to offend the senator, Morgan accepted his hand and followed him onto the dance floor.

FIFTY

Trevor sat at the hotel bar, nursing the same bottle of beer for the past hour. He wasn't much of a drinker, especially while on the job. In fact, he held little respect for people like Terrance Yeager and Urban Blair who often allowed alcohol to cloud their judgment.

When Sofia dashed out of the banquet hall earlier, Trevor was thankful to have been in the gift shop. He watched her make a call, down what looked to be an ample portion of whisky, and calmly return to the event.

He promptly called J.R. to report the unusual behavior and learned the reason for her panic: the arrival of Urban. No one expected the distraught husband to sober up long enough to attend the fundraiser, especially with his distaste for black-tie events.

Now that Sofia knew he was in the vicinity, Trevor no longer saw any reason for stealth. He didn't care if Max, Terrance, or Urban spotted him lurking about. They would assume correctly that he was on the property to protect Sofia should the need arise. J.R. had been nervous about sending her into a building swarming with security, despite her frequent contact with this crowd in the conduct of her job as a lobbyist.

The evening started out as a simple assignment, to look after a woman who wanted no protection. Unfortunately, the night was becoming more complex as the hours passed. If Urban or Terrance stepped out of line, he was to eliminate the problem, preferably in a way that looked accidental.

Trevor didn't give law enforcement a lot of credit, but even the most inept investigator would be unlikely to view Urban's death as an accident after his wife's demise. And if circumstances required that both men needed removing, chaos would surely erupt. One death at a party could be an accident, two accidents would be nearly impossible to orchestrate. But, orders were orders, and he would do J.R.'s bidding even if he didn't agree with the methods or share his confidence in the likelihood of success. J.R. paid enough to buy anyone's complete loyalty, and Trevor had no desire to step off of the gravy train.

If he and Sofia hadn't gotten off to such a rocky start, maybe he could understand his boss's fascination with her. She was beautiful, mysterious, smart, classy, and possessed back-alley skills that intrigued him. Unfortunately, he found it difficult to erase the memory of her getting the jump on him during their first encounter or the spike heel of her shoe digging into his skin. He would never forget or forgive.

As if summoned by his thoughts, Sofia exited the banquet hall. She was heading in the direction of the women's restroom at a harried pace. Setting down his beer, he threw a bill on the bar and followed at a discrete distance. As expected, she entered the ladies' room.

Scanning the dimly lit hallway, he spotted an exit leading out into the alley. He also spied a second door about halfway between the restroom and the exit. He tried the knob. It was locked, but it took him only seconds to pick the lock and slip inside.

Pulling out a tiny flashlight, he scanned the interior. The small space was a well-organized janitor's closet with the usual assortment of cleaning tools and supplies. The overpowering and unpleasant odors of sour mop water and pine-scented cleaners assaulted his senses, making him hope Sofia didn't stay in the restroom long.

Clicking off his light, he cracked the door enough to be able to spot her when she left, and to get a little fresh air. Despite the stench in the closet he would wait as long as it took to ensure he stayed close to Sofia. If anything happened to her, his lucrative career would end.

FIFTY-ONE

"You and mother seemed to be hitting it off," Senator Grant stated as he placed one hand in the small of Morgan's back and her other in his, while pulling her toward him.

Morgan thought he was holding her too close, but she didn't pull away, certain he would be more likely to talk if she played along.

"She started coughing, and I wanted to make sure she wasn't choking," Morgan replied, explaining why she had moved to the seat next to his mother.

"I hope she's OK."

"I offered to get your father or a staffer, but she assured me she'd be fine."

As the senator led her around the floor, Morgan wondered if Nick was watching. The idea made her uncomfortable. Even though this was not a social encounter, she still didn't like being in the arms of another man.

"I doubt we'll have time to talk about your future business endeavors this evening, but if you're in town for a few days, maybe we can get together somewhere more private and see what we can do for each other."

Seriously? That wasn't even subtle. "I'm afraid I fly out in the morning. Maybe another time?"

"I hope so. I'm confident we could work quite well together."

He pulled her even closer and Morgan fought the urge to stomp on his foot. She tried to lean back to insert a little distance between them, but he held firm.

"I assume you mean that if I contribute to your campaign you'll listen to my concerns, which may fall within your purview to influence as the chair of the Senate Committee on Health, Education, Labor, and Pensions?"

"Yes, among other things. There are many ways we can benefit each other," he said with a look Morgan could only interpret as a hungry leer.

As the music ebbed, Morgan quickly stepped out of his embrace. She spotted the lecherous old man from earlier heading in her direction, and she was in no mood for another dance or to be groped inappropriately by another man.

"Thank you for the dance. If you'll excuse me, I need to go and freshen up."

Morgan didn't even wait for his reply as she slipped into the crowd, effectively evading the old man and making her way out of the banquet hall. Following the signs, she walked toward the ladies' room as quickly as she could without appearing distressed. She burst through the door and nearly collided with a woman exiting the restroom.

"Sorry, excuse me," Morgan stated.

Their eyes locked. Everything about this woman had changed, yet nothing. Her eye color, hair color, hair style, and clothing were different, but the empty ruthless glare shook Morgan to her core. Morgan had no doubt who this woman was. She struggled to maintain her composure.

"I for...for...forgot my purse," Morgan stuttered as she took a small step backward.

The woman most recently known to Morgan as Candace was too fast. Like a striking snake, the woman grasped Morgan's wrist and yanked her into the restroom. She spun Morgan around, twisting her arm painfully high behind her back. Candace's other hand clamped over Morgan's mouth.

Morgan clawed at the hand covering her mouth with her free hand, but the woman's grasp was solid, and her strength didn't waiver. Candace shoved Morgan into a stall. Morgan hit the back wall of the stall head-on with so much force she nearly blacked out and feared the impact had broken her nose. Blood trickled down to her lip as she fought to regain her balance.

Before Morgan could gather her wits, Candace flipped Morgan around until they faced each other. Using her weight, Candace trapped Morgan's free arm between their bodies and kept the other pinned between Morgan's back and the cold tile wall.

Tears welled in Morgan's eyes as pain shot through her shoulder due to the pressure of Candace immobilizing her arm behind her. Was Devyn watching? Would she just see a screen filled with black from Candace's dress, or would she detect trouble?

For a moment, the woman examined every inch of her body as if searching for something. Morgan realized what she was looking for when the broach was ripped from her dress and set on top of the toilet paper dispenser facing the stall door. Candace then reached down the neck of her dress and retrieved the wire as if she knew exactly where to look, dropped the tiny device in the toilet, and flushed.

With her only hope of summoning help gone, Morgan feared for her life. This woman had let her live once, but Morgan doubted she would be so lucky a second time.

"I'm going to remove my hand, but if you scream I'll kill you."

Morgan believed the woman, so she nodded her head, indicating she understood.

"What are you doing here?" the woman hissed.

"Attending Senator Grant's fundraising event," Morgan's voice quivered.

"Wearing a wire and a camera? Bull. Who are you with?"

"I came with a childhood friend."

Morgan wondered if Devyn had been watching and prayed she'd detected the struggle on the tiny camera in the broach before Candace removed it from her dress. It had all happened so fast and for most of the time, Candace was behind her. Her movements over the past few minutes had to have appeared erratic, but were they enough to trigger suspicion?

"Never mind. You're obviously with the FBI again, so we're leaving now."

Candace's fingers dug into Morgan's arm as she nearly dragged her out of the restroom. Morgan saw no one, so decided not to test Candace's threat of death by calling out for help when there might not be anyone close enough to reach her before she died.

As Candace pushed her toward the exit sign at the end of the hall, Morgan knew her chances of survival would be reduced if she left the building. Morgan tried to pull free, but Candace held firm. She continued to struggle, digging in her heels to slow the progression. As she pulled back with all her strength, Candance suddenly released her, sending her tumbling to the floor.

Pain clouded Morgan's vision as Candace yanked her to her feet by her hair and slapped her hard across the face. Candace shoved her so hard in the back toward the exit that the force of the collision opened the door and sent Morgan tumbling into the alley.

Morgan struggled to her feet. She lamented the realization she might never see Nick again. The thought brought tears to her eyes. She tried to get her emotions under control. If she had any hopes of surviving this notorious and brutal woman a second time, she needed to clear her head and think. She couldn't gain her freedom by force, so if an opportunity to escape presented itself she had to be ready to act decisively. Her life depended on it.

FIFTY-TWO

Trevor watched as Sofia yanked the brunette back into the restroom. He debated about whether or not he should follow. He couldn't imagine Sofia was in any danger from this woman, and clearly, Sofia held the upper hand. He would wait, watch, and see how it played out.

He didn't have long to contemplate his next move when he spied Sofia and the woman hustle by. The woman was going along against her will. Sofia's intention was to leave the building through the nearby exit. The back alley wasn't being covered by security, and no alarm would go off when they opened the door. He had scoped out the alley and disabled all the alarms earlier in the day in case he needed to make a quiet escape.

As soon as Sofia and the woman disappeared out the exit, footsteps rounded the corner. He quietly shut the door expecting a woman to enter the restroom, and then he would follow Sofia. Instead, the footfalls became heavier, likely that of a man, and passed by the restroom.

"Don't run from me," the man shouted toward the closing exit.

Once the steps passed, Trevor opened the closet door just in time to watch Urban dash out of the building in pursuit of Sofia. He was certain the brunette posed no physical threat to Sofia, but he wasn't so sure about Urban. If the drunk and distraught widower believed Sofia was in anyway responsible for his wife's death, he would want revenge.

Trevor scanned the hall to make sure Urban's shout hadn't drawn attention. The hall remained quiet and empty, so he slipped out of the closet and followed Urban into the ally.

~*~

"Sofia."

She stopped and turned in response to her name being called. She couldn't believe her bad luck. She intended to fix the problem with this woman for good, but Urban's presence only complicated matters.

"What do you want?" Sofia demanded.

"I want you to pay for what you did to Margaret. She didn't deserve to die. She didn't know anything. How could you be so cold and callous? You are pure evil."

"I doubt you will believe me, but I didn't kill your wife. All I know about it is what I've read in the newspapers."

"It had to be you. Margaret was always in control. She never had accidents and would never take her own life. Someone did this to her, and it had to be you. You killed your own mentee, so you would have no problem silencing my beloved Margaret."

Sofia stared at Urban as he held a gun in his unsteady hand. As she watched the emotion play over his face, she couldn't help but pity him. She had never loved anyone the way he clearly loved his wife. Her feelings for J.R. were so complex that there was no comparison.

"Can we talk about this later? I have a little problem here I need to take care of right now." Sofia nodded toward Morgan. "This woman's presence is a very bad omen. If we don't get out of here immediately, I suspect the FBI will be crawling all over us in a matter of minutes."

"No. It can't wait. You need to pay for what you did."

"Put the gun down. You're not steady enough to hit me without taking out this woman. She has some tie to the FBI. You're not clever enough to cover your tracks. If you shoot her, they'll hunt you down. You'll spend the rest of your life in prison."

"I don't care what happens to me."

"I can prove I was nowhere near New Mexico when Margaret died. Go back to the event, and we can talk tomorrow."

"I'm done talking. I want out, and if going to prison is my only way, I'll take it."

"He'll find you. Prison won't be able to protect you."

"So be it. At least I'll be with Margaret," Urban stated as he took several steps toward the women and steadied the pistol.

Sofia pulled Morgan in front of her to shield herself with the other woman's trembling body. She looked Urban in the eyes, took a deep breath, and braced herself for the impact. At this distance, it was likely the bullet would go through Morgan's body, but she wasn't certain if it would kill them both. She couldn't determine the caliber of the weapon in the dim lighting but hoped it was small.

Testing Urban to determine if he would lose his nerve, create a moving target, and to put distance between them, Sofia slowly stepped backward pulling Morgan with her.

"Don't take another..."

Sofia halted. Urban never finished his sentence as he suddenly crumpled to the ground in a lifeless heap. She clamped a hand over Morgan's mouth to muffle the scream she expected to come from witnessing the grisly scene in front of them.

Scanning the dark reaches of the alley, she saw movement.

Trevor emerged from the shadows, offering no relief. He walked toward her, his pistol limp at his side. Unarmed, Sofia wasn't sure what she could do to protect herself if he intended to kill her, too.

Trevor stopped in front of her within arm's reach. She caught and held his gaze. She couldn't read his intentions, but the longer they stood there, the more certain she was that he didn't come to kill her.

He reached out and ripped Morgan from her grasp.

"Great. Another complication," he hissed.

"She was in Arizona with FBI agents. This couldn't be a coincidence, and she was wearing a camera and a wire," Sofia replied.

"No, I'm sure it's not. Get out of here. I'll take care of her."

"Why?"

"I didn't lie to you. I was brought to D.C. to protect you, and my orders are for you to survive and escape capture at all costs. Go now. Head that way and a car will find you," he said, titling his head in the direction he meant.

Sofia saw no point in arguing. With one last look at Trevor, she turned and ran, quickly disappearing into the night.

FIFTY-THREE

Devyn stood in line at the coffee shop with three cups of coffee in a caddy and a bag of donuts to satisfy Gordo's sweet tooth. She could see the front entrance of the hotel through the shop window. She was so focused on watching the activity that the sound of Gordo's voice made her drop the bag and grab for her ear.

"We may have a problem. Morgan's camera was jolting around. It then steadied on the stall door of the restroom, so Fitz and I respectfully turned the volume off and looked away for a few minutes. When we went back, the camera was still focused on the stall door, and when we turned the volume up, the feed was dead. We can't hear anything."

"Call Nick and tell him what you just told me. I'll go check the ladies' restroom and get back to you."

Devyn set the caddy on the counter, apologized to the clerk as she handed him a twenty, and darted across the street. She slowed as she entered the front of the hotel. She followed the signs toward the event. As she neared the double doors leading into the banquet hall she was stopped by a security guard who asked for her identification. It wasn't much, but at least he probably kept any uninvited reporters out of the event. She showed her badge, and he nodded.

"Which way to the ladies' room?"

"Past the banquet hall, then take your first left.

Can't miss it. The restroom is the only facility down that hallway."

Devyn took off at a quick pace. She was hesitant to break into a jog and attract attention over what she hoped was Morgan having a bad reaction to spoiled caviar and a malfunctioning wire.

When Devyn entered the restroom, she spotted two women standing in front of the mirror, gossiping and touching up their makeup. A quick scan under the doors told Devyn no one else was in the restroom.

"Is the camera still focused on the inside of a stall door?"

The two women turned around and gaped at her, but she ignored them.

"Yes," Gordo replied.

Devyn's heart pounded in her chest, and she gasped for a breath. This couldn't be happening again. Something was drastically wrong. She pushed open the first door, nothing. Making her way down the line, she froze at the site behind the fourth door. Morgan's broach rested on the toilet paper dispenser. Scanning the stall for other clues, she spotted a smear of blood down the back wall and drops of blood leading out of the stall.

"Call Nick, tell him where I am and that Morgan's gone. Tell him to seal the building so no one gets out. Patch him into this feed so I can talk to him directly."

Devyn raced out of the ladies' room, skidding to a stop in the hall. Spotting the exit sign and random crimson drops on the carpet, she had no doubt which direction Morgan went, or was taken.

FIFTY-FOUR

Max located Terrance on the other side of the banquet hall talking to a pretty blonde. He wove his way through the crowd toward Terrance, keeping an eye out for any sign of Urban or Sofia.

"Sorry to interrupt, but I need a word with you," Max stated as he grabbed Terrance by the arm and pulled him away from the confused young woman.

"Where's Urban?" Max demanded.

"Last I saw, he was with you," Terrance replied.

"He said he was going to talk to you and headed your way."

"Well he never made it. What's the big deal?"

Max scanned the room again and saw no sign of Urban or Sofia. He looked back at Terrance who was watching him with concern.

"We've got to find him immediately before something bad happens. He thinks Sofia killed Margaret."

"Did she?" Terrance asked.

"Claims she didn't and I tend to believe her. She said Trevor went missing the day before it happened, and she hasn't seen him since, but we've learned from J.R. that he's here on the property."

"Great. That doesn't make me feel any safer. That guy gives me the creeps. He's got no soul. You look into his eyes, and there's nothing there."

"True, but what matters at the moment is Urban

believes Sofia murdered his wife, and he wants revenge. He knows she's here, which I assume is the reason he came tonight. Now he's missing along with Sofia. If anything happens to her, J.R. will go insane. For some reason, he's totally infatuated with her."

"How can we be blamed if Urban goes after Sofia?" Terrance asked.

"Because I'm supposed to be babysitting Urban to keep him away from Sofia, and the main reason she's even here is to keep an eye on you per J.R.'s orders. He thinks you talk too much when you drink, and that made him very nervous in this crowd."

"I wouldn't worry as much about Sofia as I would about Urban. Hopefully she's discreet. A dead body shows up and everyone on the guest list will likely get grilled and investigated," Terrance replied.

Max hadn't thought of that, but now that Terrance mentioned it, he was reminded of why he always advocated to keep their distance from each other and their business dealings separate. Every remaining member of Coterie was on the guest list and present except for J.R. If someone made the connections they would all go down.

"You check the men's room, and I'll check the lobby and bar," Max stated. "We better find Urban and keep him under control. If he touches one hair on Sofia's head, we'll regret that day six years ago at the health and nutrition symposium when we formed this unholy alliance with J.R."

"I've already regretted it many times. What good is being rich if you end up dead?" Terrance said as the two men began weaving their way through the crowd toward the exit.

"I'm sorry, but we've been instructed that no one

leave this room," security said as Max reached for the door.

"We can't leave? I've got a plane to catch, and if I don't go now, I'll likely miss my flight," Max stated.

"I'm sure it won't be long, sir."

"In that case, I could use a very strong drink," Terrance stated.

"Might as well join you," Max replied as the two men left the security guard at the door and headed for the bar. "Being as how it may be our last," Max mumbled.

FIFTY-FIVE

As Devyn pushed through the exit, she spotted movement at the end of the alley. It was dark, but she was certain the shapes rounding the corner and disappearing from view belonged to a person pushing another person forward.

A quick scan of the area and she saw a body face down on the pavement in a large pool of blood. Crouching, she checked for a pulse, nothing. She rolled the body over. Urban Blair stared back at her with lifeless eyes.

"Nick, two people exited the alley on foot on the east end of the building and turned right. There's a body in the alley. Send someone back here. Gordo, pick Nick up, and I'll feed you directions. I'm going after them."

Devyn sprinted in the direction in which she spotted the people leaving the alley. As she turned the corner, she was relieved they hadn't increased the distance much. Whoever it was had Morgan. She was certain by the color of the dress and the long brunette hair swirling about during the struggle. Morgan's resistance was slowing them down and muffling any noise Devyn made as she gained on them.

Sticking to the shadows to avoid detection, Devyn whispered her status into the mic. Gordo confirmed Nick was in the van, and they were closing in on her location. She fed them the street name she was on and the direction of her travel.

"From the back, I can't confirm much. Pretty certain it's a man and a woman being escorted against her will. She's fighting which is slowing them down considerably. Trying to close the gap without drawing attention. Hurry, there's no room for error here."

After several more blocks, her quarry left the sidewalk and entered a park. Devyn quietly relayed her location back to Nick. The softer grass and closely spaced trees allowed Devyn to draw near without detection. Unfortunately, Nick would need to abandoned Gordo, Fitz, and the van soon. He would be on foot and several minutes behind her. She was on her own.

The man was clearly familiar with the park, moving with purpose and no hesitation. As the artificial lighting became scarcer and the vegetation increased, Devyn feared she might lose them. She pushed through several shrubs and found herself at the shore of a small manmade pond.

Her heart raced as panic started setting in. She couldn't lose Morgan again, but she wasn't sure which way they went. There was no path, and the pond made it necessary to choose a direction or start swimming, which they clearly hadn't done.

As she was ready to take a fifty-fifty gamble, Devyn spotted Morgan's black dress shoe, indicating the direction she had been taken. She picked her way through the bushes and heard thrashing and heavy breathing. No longer worried about being detected, Devyn picked up her pace. Forcing her way through the vegetation, she nearly collided with the man's back.

The man's hands were clasped around Morgan's throat making it impossible for her to scream.

Morgan's fingernails were clawing at the hands squeezing her neck and she was kicking wildly. Despite the efforts she was clearly doing little damage in her current position though the distraction prevented the man from noticing Devyn's arrival.

Devyn stowed her gun, unable to discharge a round with Morgan so close. She leapt up and brought her elbow down near the back of the man's neck with all the force she could muster. The impact was enough to make him release his grip on Morgan's throat.

Morgan stumbled back and fell to the ground, gasping for breath. She crawled away.

The big man went down but grabbed Devyn's ankle as he fell, taking her with him to the ground. Before she could react, he pounced on her and pinned her arms under his knees.

Devyn bucked and squirmed, trying to dislodge the massive bulk. She was clearly out-matched, and helpless in her current position.

The man backhanded Deyvn across her cheek. She struggled to keep from blacking out as she braced herself for another blow.

The heel of Morgan's remaining shoe came down hard on the man's head.

He fell to the side, allowing Devyn to scramble to her feet and out of his reach.

He grabbed his head with one hand, cursing violently, while his other hand shot out towards Morgan.

Morgan leapt back, narrowly missing being ensnared.

"Go! I mean it. Go now!" Devyn screamed at Morgan.

Morgan hesitated, then ran.

The man struggled to gain his footing, but Devyn kick out, connecting with his stomach, sending him toppling to the ground, gasping for breath. He staggered to his feet, his back toward Devyn. With his hand low on his stomach he slowly turned around until he faced her. Pulling his gun from his waistband, he raised his arm and took aim at Morgan.

With no other option, Devyn drew her Glock and fired. Once again, she would get no answers.

FIFTY-SIX

Once out of the alley, Sofia slowed to a brisk walk to avoid drawing attention. She strolled down the sidewalk against traffic in the direction Trevor had indicated. She wasn't sure what the plan was, but before long, a car she didn't recognize rolled to a stop across the street. The darkly tinted window on the driver's side eased down. She looked over.

J.R. smiled and nodded.

Dodging speeding cars and ignoring honking horns, Sofia darted across the street. With relief, she pulled open the door and slid into the passenger seat. She exhaled as the car rolled away from the curb and into traffic.

J.R. reached over and grabbed her hand, squeezing it reassuringly and holding on. "You're safe now."

Sofia rested her head against the seat and closed her eyes. She had few choices left, and the realization made her feel trapped. She had spent her entire life relying solely on herself, but the only way to avoid death or prison would be to place her fate firmly in this man's hands. She wished she could be certain about his intentions. Despite J.R.'s proclaimed love for her, she knew it was foolish to trust a criminal.

"I'm blown. I can't stay in the city. I can't go home. I can't go to the office. I can no longer use the senator."

"Are you certain?" J.R. asked.

"Yes. The woman Aaron worked for in Phoenix,

who obviously has some ties to the FBI, was at the fundraiser. We ran into each other in the ladies' room, and she recognized me. I was in the process of dealing with her before she could talk when Urban followed us out into a back alley. Trevor showed up, silenced Urban, and took the woman. He said he would handle it, told me to leave, and I left. It wasn't a coincidence the woman was here. She was wired and wore a camera. The FBI is close."

J.R. sighed and stared straight ahead for a moment. "When they go over the guest list and dig through video surveillance of the event, the remaining members of Coterie will likely be exposed. I thought getting rid of Margaret would keep Urban away and end her relationship with the Salt Lake FBI agents. I didn't like the idea of Max and Terrance both attending, but I thought we were untouchable. I deeply regret sending you to keep an eye on Terrance. If something had happened to you, it would have caused me pain too deep to heal."

It always caught Sofia off guard when he said such things to her. Until J.R., no man had ever expressed any love or compassion for her, only the desire to use and abuse her. She couldn't decide if she believed the endearing words, or if he had an ulterior motive like all other men.

"I received a formal invitation from Senator Grant. All of the large lobbying firms were represented at the function, so my being there was logical and drew no attention. I had also played my last card with the senator to ensure his continued loyalty and service. I was anxious to ascertain if it would be enough."

"Was it?"

"We'll never know. I thought it was, but then he

whispered in my ear that the code the Polk Genetic Researcher had used for his notes had been broken, and Polk has filed for a patent for the procedure to isolate the gene previously unknown to contribute to obesity. If the procedure is approved it could eliminate genetic obesity, which has the potential to put a substantial dent in the diet product market."

"Does he have any proof?"

"I don't know if he has any evidence that we were involved in silencing the researcher or if he was merely taking a stab at leveling the playing field."

"He was probably grasping at straws. His usefulness may have run its course anyway, so think nothing else of it."

Sofia nodded agreement and closed her eyes. The evening replayed over and over in her mind. The moment Urban walked into the room, she should have left, but she thought it was more important to follow through on J.R.'s request to keep an eye on Terrance than to hide from a weak man. She also suspected Max possessed skills other than business acumen, so she thought he would be able to control Urban.

If she could have slipped out of the hotel without the woman from Phoenix recognizing her, maybe she could have disappeared and started a new life somewhere else, alone. Now, the only option was to trust J.R. Acknowledging that her choices were very limited, she opened her eyes and looked over at J.R.

"I rent a small storage unit south of Alexandria. We need to stop for a minute so I can grab a few things."

J.R. smiled. "I assumed you would have an exit strategy. Your attention to detail is one of the traits I've always admired, and that has made you so valuable to the organization."

They drove for about forty-five minutes before arriving at Sofia's storage unit. The four-foot by eight-foot unit contained only the briefcase she recently obtained and a carry-on bag. She tossed the carry-on in the trunk of the car and kept the briefcase next to her on the floor of the front passenger seat.

The case not only contained her new identity, but it held the only two items in her life with any sentimental value: her karate tournament ribbon and the antique brass letter opener Aaron had given to her for her birthday the first year he worked for her. He claimed he stole it from a very wealthy and politically connected businessman during his first burglary. He never told her whose it was, but occasionally he would wink at her before an important meeting and suggest she not open any letters. It was a silly game, but the memory made her miss him. Regrets over her involvement with Coterie flooded her mind, making it difficult to hold back the tears.

She watched J.R. out of the corner of her eye, torn between love and hate. He held her fate in his hands. At the moment, she was too tired and too full of regrets to think clearly. Any rash words or actions could backfire, so she kept silent.

After the short detour, they returned to Interstate 95 and headed south. The traffic was light this late at night. Sofia assumed they would drive all night, putting as much distance as possible between her and Washington, D.C.

"It was fun while it lasted, wasn't it? We had a good run, but now we need to look ahead to the future," J.R. stated. "I think it's time you take me up on my offer and go to Brazil and start over. I can obtain a new identity for you in forty-eight hours."

"Not necessary," she stated, patting the case resting on the floor between her feet.

"Hmm…who will she be this time—a saucy red head, a fun-loving bleach blonde, a rowdy brunette party girl?"

Sofia didn't reply as she popped the lock on the case and pulled out a pair of thick glasses and put them on. Next, she slid a retainer into her mouth giving the impression she was wearing braces, and she finished the look with a mousy brown wig cut in a bob-style. She didn't bother with changing her eye color or putting on the mask, figuring she displayed enough to make her point. She smiled.

He burst out laughing. "Ah, a naughty librarian. Very good, no one would ever guess."

"Not exactly what I was going for. I was trying for nondescript. My name is now Miranda Baxter."

"Sorry, darling, you could never be nondescript. You are far too stunning, and you carry yourself with confidence and a little hint of danger, which I find simply intoxicating."

Sofia groaned and leaned her head back on the headrest. She was tired of danger and could think of nothing more appealing at the moment than being ordinary.

FIFTY-SEVEN

Devyn, Nick, Morgan, Gordo, and Fitz all let out a collective sigh of relief as the FBI's private plane left the runway in Washington, D.C. Even though Conroy had gotten approval for their small surveillance operation from his superior in D.C. beforehand, they still had a number of questions to answer. They also realized that there were a lot of law enforcement agencies unhappy with the Salt Lake Field Office agents' involvement with Senator Grant's fundraiser.

Having a couple of bodies to deal with made everyone's job more difficult. The local FBI grilled them for hours and took possession of all of the audio and video data Gordo and Fitz gathered. Devyn wanted to fight for their evidence, but Nick advised her to play nice and let Conroy work his magic to get it back. Devyn reluctantly agreed with the promise of getting out of D.C. sooner.

Several seats ahead of her, Devyn watched Morgan snuggle tightly against Nick, his arm draped possessively around her shoulders. The bond between them was so strong it made Devyn ache for that same connection with Gage, but she worried it wasn't meant to be or that she was too flawed to deserve a normal relationship.

Devyn reeled from the fact that somehow Morgan had once again been placed in danger on her watch. She didn't see anyway Nick could blame her this time, but she still couldn't help but blame herself. She should have argued against Morgan's involvement in the operation even though it had presented a convenient and quick way to get close to the senator and it was all Morgan's idea from the start.

Maybe she had become a little jaded to the dangers associated with the job after so many years. The incident served as a brutal reminder of how dangerous her career could be. She used to thrive on the thrill of a close call, but now with Gage in her life, thinking about how one misstep could turn deadly, no longer held any appeal. Not only did she fear leaving him too soon, but the thought of losing him to his job terrified her even more.

Leaning back against the seat, Devyn closed her eyes and tried to force the brutal images of Morgan's earlier peril from her mind of that man's hands around Morgan's throat and the gun taking aim at Morgan's fleeing back. Those scenes would haunt her forever. She had witnessed a lot in her career, but this incident hit too close to home. As the events ran through her mind for the tenth time, she felt someone drop down into the seat next to her.

"Go away, Gordo. I'm in no mood to be nice, and you don't deserve to see the mean side of me. It's ugly."

"Can't argue with you there, but I owe you a huge one." Nick startled her, since she assumed it was Gordo who had come to comfort her.

"For what, nearly getting Morgan killed again?" Devyn asked.

"No. you saved her life. It wasn't your idea; it was hers. Conroy sanctioned it. I was unable to change her mind. You stayed out of the argument I couldn't win.

Morgan is an adult, a very stubborn adult, and she was determined to do this."

"My gut told me it was a bad idea, but it's hard to make a convincing argument based on a sick feeling in the pit of your stomach," Devyn said.

"I know. Remember, I had the same feeling. Morgan and I have had a long talk, and she promised to quit taking years off my life. She's agreed we don't need to be this involved in each other's work."

"If it hadn't been Morgan who had such a close call, I'd be a little more excited about the outcome. I think once we've examined everything obtained through this operation, we'll have learned a lot. We discovered Candace's true identity, Sofia Wilks. Her office and apartment are sealed off and being combed over by a topnotch forensic team as we speak. As soon as we learn the identity of the big guy I shot, I bet that will shed even more light on everything. Unfortunately, Candace, I mean Sofia, slipped away again," Devyn stated.

"I won't admit it to her, and don't you ever tell her, but Morgan's involvement ended up giving us more in a few hours than we've gotten in the last month."

"I thought the same thing, but you're right. If we tell her, she may want to help even more. We'll keep it between the two of us. Go to her. She acts tough, but this had to shake her up. It'll be a long while before those bruises around her neck fade. I'm sure every time she looks in the mirror, the terror will return. If there's anything I can do don't hesitate to ask."

"Thanks but being her friend will be enough. She thinks the world of you and cherishes your friendship."

"And you?"

"Well, tonight confirmed why there's no one I trust more with my back than you, and I hope it goes both ways," Nick stated as he stood and left.

Devyn smiled. It wasn't a mushy declaration of his undying friendship and admiration for her but realizing that she still held his trust was enough.

FIFTY-EIGHT

As the sun warmed her cheek pressed against the passenger window, Sofia slowly opened her eyes. She had fallen asleep somewhere south of the Virginia and North Carolina border. They had pulled over at a truck stop where J.R. bought a cup of coffee. With her stomach tied in knots, she decided to avoid eating or drinking anything so waited in the car. Once they were back on the road she apparently dozed off.

Sofia silently watched J.R. He focused on the Interstate but didn't look overly tense. This was a new side to this complex man. He was in charge of his empire, but he always had employees to do everything, especially the dirty work. She wasn't sure if she had ever seen him drive a car before. He always had a driver.

"Where are we?"

"Ah, you are finally awake. I was starting to worry about you. I hope you feel rested," J.R. stated as he glanced over and smiled at her.

"How long have I been asleep?"

"About five hours. We're a little over an hour north of Savannah, Georgia. A plane is waiting for us there that will take us to Canada. From Canada, we fly to Cuba. From Cuba, we fly to Brazil."

Sofia closed her eyes and rested her head against the seat. Everything had fallen apart so quickly the night before that she was finding it difficult to process.

If she could only go back in time, she would have stayed home. If she had stayed home, she would still own her freedom.

"Are you all right?" J.R. asked as he reached over and squeezed her hand.

"Physically yes, but I'm having a difficult time wrapping my mind around last night and understanding what my future holds."

"We knew the FBI was closing in when Urban saw your two alias photos on the agent's cell phone. Unfortunately, there was no way anyone could have foreseen that the woman from Arizona would be at the event and that she would recognize you. Your disguises have been foolproof until now. She must be one very observant woman."

"Both times we found ourselves in very close proximity to each other. I imagine the recognition came from more than just my appearance."

"It doesn't matter now. I'm sure the FBI will be digging through your home and office and trying to reconstruct your past. By the time they think they have a handle on who you are, you'll be long gone."

J.R.'s statement made her mind reel. She kept nothing personal at the office and very little in her apartment, but what little she possessed was hers and she was very protective of her privacy and her few belongings.

She kept one flash drive with the video of her mother's murder in her carry-on luggage in the trunk and a second copy in a bank safe deposit box under the name of Candace Rogers. The key to the box was safely on the ring in her purse. It was possible the authorities would track down the Candace Rogers safe deposit box, but it would all depend on how wide of a net they cast and how thoroughly they investigated.

When Sofia thought about her home and office being pawed through by the FBI and her past being dredge up, she couldn't hold in her emotions. She bit her lip but couldn't stop the single tear from sliding down her cheek.

"Sofia, darling, we can't change what happened last night. But the events opened up a whole new world for Miranda Baxter to explore, and I'll be with her every step of the way. We'll enjoy a wonderful life together. You must trust me."

"I buried my past. I built my life from nothing. I showed only what I wanted to show. I was in total control of my life and my destiny. Now I've been left with nothing."

"You have me."

Sofia tried to smile. She wanted to believe he was sincere, but doubts plagued her. Now that she was completely dependent upon him for her survival, would that change his feelings for her? Would he still respect her or would he think of her as simply another one of his many possessions? "Thank you. The fact that you came to my rescue in person rather than sending another Trevor-like goon means a lot to me."

"You are most precious to me. I could not trust your escape from the city and your safety to anyone else. I have not always been a business man. I do possess a few skills of my own. I just normally prefer to avoid getting my hands dirty, so to speak. Always remember that I love you more than anything else in my life."

Sofia didn't know what else to say. He probably wanted her to say she loved him, too, but she wasn't sure if she could. Not experiencing any love growing up, she didn't trust herself to recognize the signs. His declarations of love and devotion should have brought her comfort, but they only made her feel uneasy, trapped, and afraid.

FIFTY-NINE

Devyn wasn't sure what to expect when she, Nick, Gordo, Fitz, and Morgan assembled in the briefing room at Conroy's request. She believed, with the exception of Morgan's near-miss, that the operation was a success, but would he agree? Despite getting pre-approval from Washington, they still had a lot of explaining to do after the fact.

"First, I want to thank Morgan, and apologize to Nick and Morgan for everything that happened in D.C. Clearly, we had no idea Morgan would come face-to-face with Sofia Wilks, the woman behind Candace and Janice. I'm impressed that Morgan was able to recognize her without either of her previous disguises since it required some pretty sophisticated facial recognition software to even connect Candace and Janice," Agent Gerald Conroy stated.

"Imagine my surprise," Morgan added. "She looked so different, yet everything about her was so familiar. When she grabbed me and pulled me into the restroom, the feel of her finger tips digging into my skin again sent my mind reeling back to that crowded stairwell in the Phoenix hospital. I feared she had no intention of letting me live since I'd be able to expose her true identity, but I never gave up hope that Nick and Devyn would find me in time."

"I can't tell you how sorry I am, and I'll beat myself up for that decision for a long time. Bottom line,

I shouldn't have allowed you to be put in that position. Unfortunately, we can't undo what happened, but we can take what we learned and put an end to this deranged organization once and for all. If we round up all the players and put them behind bars, your sacrifice will have meant something huge—you may have helped save a lot of innocent lives gauging by the number of victims so far."

"I'm glad I could help, but I believe my career in law enforcement is very short lived. I have no desire to get that close to death again. Did you learn the identity of the man who tried to strangle me or his connection to Sofia?"

Devyn focused on Conroy as he explained that the man's name was Trevor Montoya and that he showed up to fill in for Sofia's previous assistant, Justine, who had been murdered while out jogging a month earlier. Sofia's current assistant, Kelly, was all too happy to discuss how much the staff disliked and feared Trevor, and she believed that Ms. Wilks did not want him around either and his presence seemed to make her nervous as well.

"If what her assistant said is accurate, it makes me wonder what he was doing at Buyers Choice Foundation in the first place," Devyn asked.

"I think I can help with that," Morgan interjected. "When Trevor yanked me out of Sofia's grasp he said something to the effect that he hadn't lied to her. He said he was sent to D.C. to protect her and that his orders were for her to survive and escape capture at all costs. He then told her a car would find her and that he'd take care of me, which we all know what that meant."

Devyn stood up and grabbed an erasable marker.

On the whiteboard she scribbled the word Coterie at the top and underlined the word. Below Coterie she jotted, "Sofia's protector." Below that she wrote Sofia Wilks, Urban Blair, and Preston Hoyle next to each other.

"What about Aaron, Trevor, and the senator?" Gordo asked.

"I don't think Aaron and Trevor were members or that the senator is currently involved with Coterie. They were hired guns or useful pawns. We know Sofia killed Aaron, and likely she or Trevor killed Urban. We learned that Sofia was a lobbyist, who in all likelihood was blackmailing the senator to influence issues impacting the diet product industries. Between interviewing Sofia's staff and the senator, I think we can verify these assumptions. Urban and Preston both owned companies that profited immensely from the manipulation of the diet, health, nutrition, medical research, and pharmaceutical industries. Aaron's past was obscure and pretty shady. He had nothing to gain from keeping people hooked on diet products. We've yet to uncover anything about Trevor, but it's safe to say he wasn't a businessman, more likely a hired thug sent to protect Sofia."

"Makes sense, but how can we be certain your membership list is complete and how do we find out who Sofia's protector is?" Nick asked.

"We go through the senator's invitee list and check if there is anyone else who would benefit from manipulating the diet product industries. I also believe Urban told me who Sofia's protector is," Devyn replied.

Devyn smiled at all the stunned looks from around the table. Maybe she was making a huge leap, but she felt she was on to something.

"When Urban was slurring and sobbing, I thought he said, 'jars sofa mess pay.' Clearly from what Morgan told us about the exchange between Urban and Sofia in the alley, he believed Sofia killed his wife, so I think he was saying, 'jars Sofia must pay.'"

"Real helpful, any idea who Jars is? A last name would be nice, or do you think that's his or her first name?" Nick asked.

Devyn sighed. "Do I have to figure everything out around here? I thought we were supposed to be a team."

"OK, unless anyone has something new to add, I think we're all up to speed on what we learned from this mission," Conroy said. "Gordo and Fitz run 'Jars,' J.R.s, and any other combos you can think of through the system and see if you can come up with anything, especially if you can make a connection to any of the industries related to the Risky Research investigation. I'll ask D.C. to follow-up with Sofia's staff on whether or not Sofia was in the area during the time of Margaret Blair's death. Devyn, get the list of invitees and check if any others on the list would benefit from manipulating the diet and nutritional products market. I'll work on the D.C. FBI to get Gordo and Fitz access to the audio and video footage they gathered at the event and any other evidence obtained as a result of the follow-up investigation. Once we get the video we'll look for anyone talking to Urban for more than just a friendly greeting. Nick and Morgan go home and get ready for your wedding. I don't want to see either one of you until Saturday afternoon at the chapel."

Devyn accepted that the meeting was over when Conroy left the briefing room. For a moment, the remaining group sat in silence pondering what they had learned and how to tackle Conroy's assignments. Devyn realized they obtained a mountain of new data to plow through, but she was confident they would find more answers.

"I sure hope one of these leads pans out before another body shows up," Nick finally stated, breaking the silence. "I don't like the idea that the woman who has tried twice to kill Morgan is still out there."

"Well, that may be stretching it a bit. She could have easily killed me in Arizona, and she never actually got the chance in D.C.," Morgan stated.

"That doesn't make me feel better," Nick added.

"I think we may see a sharp drop in the body count. Why go after Morgan now? Sofia has to realize her cover is blown and that every law enforcement agency in the country is looking for her. Not that I don't think you two shouldn't be joined at the hip until we track her down. Coterie is probably down by at least two members and obviously we're on to them. If I were a betting woman, I'd say they'll lay low for a while to lick their wounds and regroup. We still need to round them up and put them out of business once and for all but, hopefully, they'll take a vacation from killing for a while," Devyn speculated.

"I hope your right," Nick added, "because they've been hitting way too close to home."

SIXTY

A gentle nudge on Sofia's shoulder brought her out of a sleep plagued with nightmares of Trevor chasing her through the dense steaming jungles of Brazil, wielding a machete as long as her arm, screaming her name. Looking around nervously, she struggled to get her bearings and her breathing under control.

The adoring smile on J.R.'s face did little to ease her apprehension. She sat in a plush leather seat in a small plane next to a ruthless man who claimed to love her, leaving behind the only life she had ever known in exchange for an existence of uncertainty in a country she had never set foot in.

The only bright spot was that Trevor was not on the plane. She wouldn't mourn the loss if he had been captured or killed by the FBI but doubted she could be so lucky. Now that it no longer mattered to her personally, she hoped the woman had survived and Trevor had not. So far, J.R.'s sources were unable to provide any information on the status of Trevor or the investigation.

"Are we there?" Sofia asked as she pushed herself up in her seat and rubbed the grit from her eyes.

"We're about thirty minutes from landing in Brazil, but we need to talk about a few things before we land, so I'm glad you're awake."

Sofia nodded and accepted the glass of water he

held out to her.

"First, in my business dealings in Puerto Rico and in Brazil I am only known by my given name. You must address me as either Jacoby or Mr. Rivera from now on. I used J.R. with Coterie to avoid giving my real name, but the two should never be used in the same circle. Only you and Max know my true identity."

"I'm sure Preston, Urban, and Terrance were all too lazy, greedy, and inept to try and find out," Sofia mumbled.

J.R. chuckled. "My thoughts exactly, but Max is different. We met while he was serving as an Army pilot at Ft. Buchanan in Puerto Rico, training pilots for the Puerto Rican Air National Guard. For a military man, he frequented some pretty exclusive night clubs, and we struck up a friendship. I could tell instantly that he possessed a unique skill set and a desire for a much higher standard of living than a military career could provide. He had an amazing aptitude for business and the fortitude to do what was necessary to get things done. He took care of a few unpleasant tasks for me in Puerto Rico, and when he got out of the military, I loaned him the funds he needed to get started in business. Clearly his talent for investing and his affiliation with Coterie helped make him very successful."

Sofia didn't ask what "unpleasant tasks" Max had taken care of for J.R., but she was now seeing Max in a different light. She knew he was shrewd but assumed his and J.R.'s association was solely about money like the rest. She made a mental note to not cross Max again or underestimate him.

"If he has such 'unique skills,' why was I sent so

often to clean up everyone's messes or to ensure a successful outcome?"

"You exhibit more finesse. Max is less subtle and brute force is not always the best method, especially when it's information we seek. I doubt he could have slipped into companies as seamlessly as you. You're a natural and a very effective chameleon."

"Will Max be joining us in Brazil?"

"No, at least not right away. There are a few things I need him to address first."

"And Terrance?"

"He has nothing left to offer. He will be dealt with as necessary."

Sofia feared what would be "necessary" for a member of Coterie who had "nothing left to offer," especially if she now fell into that category.

"We've escaped, so what can Terrance do to hurt us?" Sofia couldn't believe she was defending Terrance, but she was tired of all the killing.

"You escaped. I still own businesses and many assets in Puerto Rico and Miami. I don't want to lose my freedom to travel at will."

"He doesn't even know your real name."

"Yes, but if he leads the authorities to my compound in Miami, it won't take them long to figure it out even though the property was purchased in the name of a shell corporation. Don't fret about Terrance. He has no one. He won't be missed."

The statement hit Sofia like a punch to the gut. She had no one and wouldn't be missed so how could she expect a different outcome to her life? She needed to shake off the self-pity and emotional tidal wave she was riding and focus on survival. She would get settled and excel in her new job. When he became comfortable that she accepted her new life, she would figure out a way to disappear before it was too late.

"One last thing," J.R. said, interrupting her thoughts. "Now that your true identity is known and the authorities are investigating every aspect of your life, will the information you've been holding over the senator come to light?"

She was a little surprised by the question and thought for a minute before answering. The affair was likely to come out, but she doubted the murder would since she and Carson Grant were the only persons privy to the truth. It was possible the last thumb drive would be located, and she didn't care if it was. She actually hoped the FBI would find the recording and the Grants would pay for ruining lives.

"Some of it, maybe, though I hope it all comes out. The Grant men deserve nothing less."

"Then share your secret with me."

"Why?"

"You never know when it may come in handy."

"I thought we were done with Coterie and Senator Grant, moving on, looking to the future."

J.R. shrugged. "For the most part, but I want you to trust me enough to share your deepest secrets."

He was testing her. There was no good reason not to tell him, but it was her secret to hold, the one thing which still belonged to her and to no one else. If she refused to tell him would there be consequences? Would he lose his faith in her? She needed to gain his trust in order to facilitate her eventual escape. Her mind whirled, trying to come up with an answer.

"Please be seated and fasten your seatbelts. We're starting our decent into Rio de Janeiro and will be landing shortly."

The pilot's voice over the intercom rescued Sofia from having to answer. The four-person flight crew on the chartered jet joined Sofia and J.R. and moved about to prepare for landing, ending their current discussion. The plane was not J.R.'s, nor was its crew, so as long as they remained close by Sofia had been granted a reprieve from having to share her secret.

Doing as instructed, Sofia fastened her seatbelt and stowed her briefcase under the seat in front of her. She handed her empty water glass to one of the attendants, rested her head back, and closed her eyes. She had never been fond of flying, especially take-off and landing, so she did not resist when J.R. took her hand.

After nearly two days of hopping around airports and private airstrips in multiple countries, Sofia was relieved to finally be in Brazil. As she stepped outside the airport she was slapped by stifling humid heat. It reminded her of Florida, but worse. It would take some time getting used to her new home, and to adjust to being at the mercy of a ruthless man who claimed to love her.

"Come, Miranda, darling. Let's go to my home and freshen up from all this travel."

It took Sofia a moment to realize he was talking to her. She had used other identities many times before, but always knew she would eventually be Sofia Wilks again. This time it was permanent. She had to leave her former self behind forever. She wasn't sure that was so bad. No one would miss Sofia Wilks. She wasn't a very good person. Maybe Miranda could be better.

"After we shower, rest, and get some dinner, I'll give you a tour of the new pharmaceutical plant. It is amazing. We've incorporated the most current technology available into all aspects of the facility from management to production to distribution. I'm sure you will be quite impressed."

She couldn't believe his enthusiasm. He had masterfully orchestrated her escape from the United States and her entry into Brazil. Everything proceeded smoothly, with no questions asked. He behaved as if they were embarking on a wonderful journey together rather than running for her life. If she would have been arrested she would have spent the rest of her life in prison or may have been executed, if she were lucky. Spending her life in a cage would be a far worse punishment than death.

"Miranda, you must not look so sad. Embrace the beginning of the rest of your life. We will be so good together. You will see."

Sofia tried to smile to mask the sadness and fear consuming her.

SIXTY-ONE

Devyn was relieved the week was about over. She had been so optimistic when they returned to Salt Lake that the remaining pieces would start falling into place and they would finally solve the Risky Research cases. Instead, that all-too-familiar feeling of hitting one brick wall after another persisted.

The Washington D.C. office continued to ignore Agent Conroy's requests to share the evidence collected during their surveillance operation. They refused to divulge the status of their investigation or provide a timeline on when they might release information.

She assumed they were being extra cautious and tight-lipped due to Senator Carson Grant's possible involvement and fear of his stable of lawyers, which made her want to scream. The longer Sofia Wilks and the rest of Coterie remained at large, the greater the risk that someone else might die.

Devyn was convinced that the senator was not a member of Coterie, just a pawn being blackmailed by Sofia. She wasn't sure if discovering what Coterie or Sofia held over him would help the investigation, but she wanted to find out nonetheless.

"Hey, Devyn, Conroy wants to see us in his office," Gordo stated as he and Fitz approached.

"What's he want?"

"Don't know. He just said get Devyn and come to

my office ASAP," Gordo replied.

Pushing herself out of her chair, she groaned. Most of the progress she'd made on healing her body after Arizona came undone when she tackled Trevor in the park. Once again, her aches and pains made her feel twice her age. Hoping Conroy had good news, she followed the two young men into their boss's office.

"Take a seat. I finally heard back from my superior in D.C. As you can imagine, they need to tread lightly in matters involving high-level politicians since much of their budgets and many of their jobs are at the mercy of these same individuals."

"So, are we getting the evidence or not?" Devyn asked impatiently.

"Yes, we're getting everything but with conditions."

Devyn sighed. She assumed there'd be a catch.

"They want us to continue to lead the investigation to keep a layer between the politicians and the D.C. FBI. I imagine if we step over the line they plan to claim they weren't aware of what the field was doing. Plausible deniability," Conroy said.

"Figures. The investigation goes south and they'll throw us under the bus without hesitation," Devyn stated.

Conroy ignored her comment and continued. "The D.C. authorities are more concerned at the moment about how someone as deadly as Sofia managed to get such unrestricted access to so many politicians for so many years and how Morgan was kidnapped from the event so easily. They're buried in a politically charged after-action-review."

"How soon will they turn everything over to us?" Gordo asked. "It would be nice to finally be able to analyze the data we gathered."

"Everything should be uploaded to the Risky Research database by Monday morning. I was assured we would get our audio and video surveillance footage back as well as any hotel security or Senator Grant's private security detail recorded: the guest list, and everything they've gathered while going through Sofia Wilks' office and apartment, including the interviews with her employees. I also learned they matched Trevor's DNA to that found on Sofia's murdered assistant, Justine. He also promised to add their weight behind our request to track the money transfers into Frank the assassin's Cayman bank account."

"So, what's the catch?" Devyn asked.

"We are not to contact Senator Grant directly. If you have questions for him, those must go through the D.C. FBI. He claims he's not being blackmailed by Sofia Wilks and his only dealings with her were in her capacity of a lobbyist."

"In the meantime, did any of you turn up anything else?" Agent Conroy asked.

"The autopsy on Margaret Blair came back. No surprise, she was murdered. The only interesting piece is that I sent Sofia's and Trevor's photos to the Santa Fe police investigator. When he showed them around the spa they found several eye witnesses who placed Trevor at the facility, no one claimed to have seen Sofia," Devyn replied.

"Well, that's consistent with Sofia's staff. According to the D.C. authorities, her assistant claimed she was at the office during the time the murder occurred, so I guess Urban got it wrong and Trevor Montoya was the killer, not Sofia," Conroy stated. "Gordo, Fitz, you got anything?"

"Not much. We're searching for J.R.s in any of the Risky Research related industries, but that's yielding mountains of data. We think 'jars' is probably J.R.'s since Urban was referring to Sofia belonging to someone. Problem is J.R. is usually the initials of a person's first and middle names, like John Robert. In business, this individual likely goes by whatever those initials stand for, so we've been compiling a list of anyone in a high-level position in the diet product, nutrition, research, and pharmaceutical world whose first name starts with J. I fear we're searching for a needle in a haystack."

"Drop that line for now. Maybe you'll find something more useful in the data we should receive from D.C. by Monday. Let's call it a week, and I'll see you three at Nick's and Morgan's wedding tomorrow," Conroy stated.

The trio stood and left. Outside Conroy's office, Gordo paused. "Um, do you have a date for the wedding or do you want to go with me and Fitz?"

"Not sure yet. Gage's deputy was supposed to be back from his honeymoon, but last night he was still stuck at the Atlanta airport."

"Well, just let me know. I'd be happy to pick you up in case you want to cut loose and blow off some steam. I could be your designated driver."

"Thanks. I'll think about it."

When Devyn reached her desk, she saw two dozen red roses sitting in the middle of her desk and several women admiring the arrangement. It should have brought a smile to her face, but she assumed it was an "I'm sorry I can't make it" offering from Gage.

"Those are beautiful, who are they from?" one of the women asked.

"My guess is they're from her imaginary boyfriend," Gardner stated as he strolled up and snatched the card from the bouquet.

"Gardner, I've had a tough week. Give me the card and get out of here," Devyn demanded.

"Let's find out who Devyn's flowers are from?" Gardner announced as he held the card high in the air.

"They're from me."

The familiar deep voice seemed to silence the entire floor. Not a word was spoken as Gardner slowly turned around to find himself eye level with the speaker's chin. Devyn almost squeaked with joy as she watched Gardner's expression change from a snarky sneer to confusion and concern.

Gage ripped the card from Gardner's hand and stared the shorter man down. Gage was a good six inches taller than Gardner, with much broader shoulders and a look in his eyes that challenged Gardner to respond.

"Who are you?" Gardner's voice cracked ever so slightly making Devyn's smile grow wider.

"Gage Harris."

"The Wyoming sheriff," Gordo mumbled in awe.

"I assume you must be Gardner, because I don't see any other weasels in this room." Gage challenged.

Gardner's mouth dropped open.

"I'll take that as a yes. Devyn's been itching to teach you a lesson for being such a jerk to her and all of the new employees that come on board here. I have no doubt she can make you beg for mercy, but she hasn't wanted to let her partner down by getting suspended. I have no such problem. Do I make myself clear?"

Gardner nodded but still hadn't spoken.

"I believe you took something that isn't yours and

therefore you owe someone an apology," Gage stated as he handed the card back to Gardner.

Gardner paused and stared up at Gage. Devyn figured he was debating between looking weak in front of his colleagues or testing Gage's threat.

"I believe this belongs to you. Sorry." Gardner handed Devyn the card, rushed to his desk, grabbed his jacket, and headed for the elevator.

"Hope I didn't make matters worse?" Gage stated as he smiled down at Devyn.

"No. It's about time someone stood up to that pig. If he bothers her again all of us women that he harasses and belittles will file a joint complaint," the woman who had asked about the flowers stated.

"That's right," the one next to her added.

"Shows over. Back to work," Conroy ordered as he approached Devyn's desk.

Devyn introduced Gage to Conroy, Gordo, and Fitz, fighting to keep the uncharacteristic grin off her face. Gordo and Fitz seemed a little nervous and quickly excused themselves. Conroy wasn't so shy.

"I've heard a great deal about you, Sheriff, from Devyn and Nick. It's nice to finally meet you. We appreciate all the cooperation on the Risky Research case. If it wasn't for you and your deputy these thugs might still be operating under the radar. So, what do we owe this visit to?"

"I came down to escort Devyn to Nick's wedding and to gauge whether or not I might coax her into making a trip down the aisle one of these days."

Devyn was so stunned she couldn't speak.

"Good luck on that." Conroy chuckled. "See you tomorrow."

Conroy hadn't even missed a beat while she was

still unable to form a coherent sentence.

"Well Devyn, are you ready for a wedding?"

"Whose?"

"I believe that's up to you," he replied as he pulled her into his arms and kissed her until she was sure she would fall to the floor if he let her go.

When she finally felt oxygen returning to her brain, she put her arms around Gage's neck and looked up into his hazel eyes.

"Let's see. You took care of me when I was injured and grumpy and didn't run away. We've worked together on several big cases. You've sent me flowers, displayed acts of chivalry, and dominated all my waking thoughts for years. It may be a little backward, but I think all we're missing is a real date."

"How does dinner and a movie sound?"

"Perfect," Devyn said as she put an arm around his waist and guided him out of the building.

Thank you

We appreciate you reading this Prism title. For other
Christian fiction and clean-and-wholesome stories,
please visit our on-line bookstore at
www.prismbookgroup.com.

For questions or more information, contact us at
customer@pelicanbookgroup.com.

Prism is an imprint of
Pelican Book Group
www.PelicanBookGroup.com

Connect with Us
www.facebook.com/Pelicanbookgroup
www.twitter.com/pelicanbookgrp

To receive news and specials, subscribe to our bulletin
http://pelink.us/bulletin

May God's glory shine through
this inspirational work of fiction.

AMDG

You Can Help!

At Pelican Book Group it is our mission to entertain readers with fiction that uplifts the Gospel. It is our privilege to spend time with you awhile as you read our stories.

We believe you can help us to bring Christ into the lives of people across the globe. And you don't have to open your wallet or even leave your house!

Here are 3 simple things you can do to help us bring illuminating fiction™ to people everywhere.

1) If you enjoyed this book, write a positive review. Post it at online retailers and websites where readers gather. And share your review with us at reviews@pelicanbookgroup.com (this does give us permission to reprint your review in whole or in part.)

2) If you enjoyed this book, recommend it to a friend in person, at a book club or on social media.

3) If you have suggestions on how we can improve or expand our selection, let us know. We value your opinion. Use the contact form on our web site or e-mail us at customer@pelicanbookgroup.com

God Can Help!

Are you in need? The Almighty can do great things for you. Holy is His Name! He has mercy in every generation. He can lift up the lowly and accomplish all things. Reach out today.

Do not fear: I am with you; do not be anxious: I am your God. I will strengthen you, I will help you, I will uphold you with my victorious right hand.
~Isaiah 41:10 (NAB)

We pray daily, and we especially pray for everyone connected to Pelican Book Group—that includes you! If you have a specific need, we welcome the opportunity to pray for you. Share your needs or praise reports at http://pelink.us/pray4us

Free Book Offer

We're looking for booklovers like you to partner with us! Join our team of influencers today and periodically receive free eBooks and exclusive offers.

For more information
Visit http://pelicanbookgroup.com/booklovers